Pierre François: 5th Grade Mishaps

Lori Ann Stephens

Illustrated by
Trevor Yokochi

Second printing

ISBN: 978-1-61296-975-6
PUBLISHED BY BLACK ROSE WRITING
www.blackrosewriting.com

Printed in the United States of America
Suggested Retail Price (SRP) $16.95

*Pierre Franç*ois: 5th Grade Mishaps is printed in Permian Slab Serif

For our bests:
Mr. Solomon & Mr. Morton ~ Lori

Miss Bobbie & Mrs. Krusleski~ Trevor

Praise for Pierre:

"*Pierre Francois: 5th Grade Mishaps* is the charming tale of a French/American boy trying to navigate the baffling social currents of fifth grade. Boys and girls alike will be able to relate to Pierre's humorous misadventures at school, and they will be rooting for him to triumph over the challenges he faces in spending two nights away at Adventure Camp."

–Polly Holyoke, author of Texas Bluebonnet Award Nominee *The Neptune Project* and *The Neptune Challenge*

"*Pierre François* is great book for parents and teachers. This funny novel not only normalizes the sometimes-embarrassing ordeals and challenges that elementary-aged children face, but also highlights the importance of constructive direction and support from parents and teachers as children shape their self-esteem and identities. And it's a fun read-aloud!"

–Galit Ribakoff, M.S., Licensed Professional Counselor (LPC), National Certified Counselor

Table of Contents

CHAPTER 1

Because We Need an Introduction

MY NAME IS Pierre François.

Not Pee-air. It's *Pierre*.

But you're right if you think it sounds the same.

Pierre. *Pee-air*.

In fact, I've just said it aloud five times and it *is* the same. That isn't good. I do *not* like bathroom humor.

What I *do* like is France. Pierre is a French name, in case you don't know.

France is the best, also in case you don't know.

All my teachers tell me I'm lucky because my Papa is French, which means I get to go to Paris at Christmas to visit my grandparents. But it also means that I *have* to go. I don't get to see my best friends for two whole weeks! Mom, who is not French, reminds me I need to look at the bright side. Tell me three Bright Sides, she says.

1. My best friends are unlikely to move to Mars while I'm gone. 2. Papa lets me drink coffee in Paris. 3. Three is always hard. Well, I suppose my French name is pretty fancy.

"*Fancy*?" Bo says. Bo is my best friend since kindergarten. He's an expert at talking to animals and giving advice. "Don't say it's fancy."

"Why not?"

Bo looks at the ceiling, groans, and pushes up his glasses. We're walking to the bathroom because it's recess and melting outside. And when it's melting outside, Bo and Max and I sneak inside to make soap-bubble mountains in the boys' restroom. Max is my other best friend from kindergarten. He's an expert at drawing soldiers and girl-charming.

"Fancy is a *girl* word," Bo says.

"No, it's not," Max says.

"Yes it is," Bo says. "My sister says fancy. *I'm so fancy!*" he says like a girl.

"There's no such thing as girl-words and boy-words. That's dumb," Max says.

"You're dumb."

"You're dumber than dumb." I can hear Max's throat wobble. He's about to turn red in the face and accidentally shove Bo against the wall. I'm good at predicting these things.

Bo growls and Max's cheeks turn red. Actually, they might have been red from the billion-degree playground outside, but they're *extra* red now.

I have to stop them before things get out of control.

"Not so loud!" I grab my hair in frustration. I'd pull it out if it weren't so curly and beautiful.

Papa says it's French hair, so it can't help being beautiful.

"How about...instead of fancy..." I search for the fanciest word I know. I am, after all, an expert at using big words. "How about *sophisticated*?"

Bo and Max stare at me. Then at each other. They shrug.

"Pierre *is* pretty sophisticated," Max says.

Bo mumbles, "I still say fancy's a girl word."

We sneak past the counselor's office.

"Who cares!" I say. "Everybody thinks I'm a girl, anyway."

Bo and Max nod. They can't argue with the truth.

"Boys!" Mrs. Angler's voice stops us in our tracks. "Why are you wandering the halls? Do you have permission to be inside?"

We turn around, and Mrs. Angler is already hovering over Bo and Max. She leans over us with her squinty eyes and her old-coffee breath. Everyone knows Mrs. Angler hates boys.

"Some horrible boys have been flushing toilet paper rolls and flooding the bathrooms. Could they have been sneaking in during recess?"

I have no idea what she's talking about, but I have the suspicion we're about to be framed. I glance around us in panic, hoping my genius-brain can rescue us. But all I see is a blue-girl outline on the restroom door.

Mrs. Angler's eyes land on me and my sweaty curls. "Oh, I'm sorry, dear. I didn't mean to call you a boy." Her voice is all honey and I know what's coming. She pulls open the girls' restroom door and smiles.

Normally when a teacher does this, I smile and say, "Actually, I'm a boy." And then they turn red-cheeks and hurry away. It's hilarious.

But today, my mouth is not working because I've never been caught in the hall without a pass, and now the universe is punishing me. I might have to *actually go* into a girl's restroom.

"You were going to the restroom?" Mrs. Angler says.

I swallow and nod slowly because technically that's where we *were* going. I'm glad I've distracted Mrs. Angler the Boy Wrangler away from Bo and Max. I'm heroic that way. But I can't go into a girl's restroom. I can't. That's illegal or something.

"After you." Mrs. Angler sweeps her arm inside the restroom and waits for me.

Bo and Max stare at me with bug-eyes.

"Water...first?" is all I manage to say.

Mrs. Angler looks at Bo, then Max, then me. "Oh. Well...hurry up," she says, waving her fingers at the water fountain. She squints at us again, then hobbles into the restroom.

Of course we don't get water. We don't make soap-bubble mountains. Instead, we walk-run back out to the playground, practically shoving each other all the way. My heart is beating like crazy and I have a weird twitch pulling on my lips like I'm about to laugh because this is the third time this month that someone's opened the girl's restroom door for me. But Max and Bo aren't smiling. They're hunched over catching their breath and giving each other the stink-eye.

I smell another argument coming on, so I slap them on the shoulders and say, "We're safe. That was some fancy footwork!" It's something my mom says. Bo squints at me.

Maybe fancy *is* a girl word.

Today, practically everyone on the playground is fighting again. About Keepie Ball. It's been a whole month since school started, and let me tell you: fifth grade changes people.

Kindergarten was great. Everyone's nice when they're six. First grade, still nice. Second grade, *still* nice. Third and fourth grades, yep: nicety-nice. But the first week of fifth grade, I noticed a disturbing change. The girls were talking and *Just. Never. Stopped.* And the boys separated into two groups: the Kickballers and the Taggers. Then Tyler brought his green ball to school and made up a game called Keepie Ball, which was all the rage. It's Keepie Ball Monday, Tuesday, Wednesday, Thursday, Friday. It's out of control. That classic game Tag (my favorite, of course) has completely disappeared. I tried playing Keepie Ball, but Tyler keeps changing the rules so that everyone is happy, but somehow the opposite happens, and everyone's mad and shouts, "Unfair!" and "Cheater!"

So Morton Elementary isn't a big happy family anymore. All the boys are annoying and all the girls are mean.

Just last night, I told my mom and Papa: "I hate fifth grade. All the boys are annoying and all the girls are mean."

"That can't be true," Mom said.

"It *is* true. For instance, today. I didn't hear the teacher call on Megan to answer a question, and when I said 'I know,' all the girls turned around and shouted 'PEE-AAAIIRR!' like I was a big know-it-all or something. I can't help it if my ears don't function."

"I think your *hears* are fine, *pard'ner*," Papa said in his chewy French accent. He was trying to talk like a Texan, but it wasn't so funny. I needed sympathy.

"Well, none of the boys want to play tag anymore. They just want to play stupid Keepie Ball. Then everyone gets into a big fight about who scored what until the teachers take away the ball and everyone's all mad."

Normally Mom's pretty good at solving problems, but last night she and Papa just nodded and raised their eyebrows and clinked their glasses of wine.

"Puberty does weird things to kids," Mom said.

"Gross. I'm not talking about that. We're at the *table*." Last summer, Mom gave me a book about puberty, and let me tell you: it is not a dinner word.

"Mean girls build character, not that I personally know any mean girls, *ma jolie*," Papa said and gave Mom a wink.

"Fifth grade is a year of changes, dear," Mom said, and mussed up my hair.

Changes, yes. But I don't think it's because of puberty. I think it's aliens.

I am not kidding. My theory is that aliens landed on the Fifth Grade Wing of Morton Elementary and did some bodysnatching.

On the first day of school, while I was in the restroom trying to get the highest soap-bubble mountain ever on my palms, the Alien Mothership brainwashed all the fifth graders. Except me. Pierre the Survivor.

Bo and Max were the most unfortunate victims of the Alien Apocalypse. We used to be the Three Musketeers.

Now, Bo and Max and I can't play at each other's house at the same time. Two of us together is fine. Me and Bo. Bo and Max. Max and me. The universe is at peace. But when the three of us get together on Saturdays, someone goes home with a galactic bruise or smoke coming out of his brains. Someone named Bo or Max. Mom says I'm the mediator. I'm not exactly sure what "mediator" means, but I think it has to do with protecting your two best friends from killing each other.

Even though they may have been body-snatched by aliens, I'm glad that Bo and Max mostly get along at school because—did I mention?– everyone else in the fifth grade has moved to the state of Ill-annoying.

ᐤᐤᐤ

Fifth grade does have its benefits, though, and Adventure Camp is number one on the list. We've all been waiting for Adventure Camp since kindergarten. Maybe that's why we're all grumpy.

"Class," Mrs. Dixie claps her hands. "Do you all remember what we did in Science during our first week this year?"

I raise my hand, but Mrs. Dixie calls on Max.

"We dissected an owl pellet with our bare hands."

"That's right."

I add more detail, because Mrs. Dixie says details are important. "I found a dozen tiny rodent skulls in that little vomit ball."

Megan turns around and holds her nose at me. "That's gross, Pee-air."

"It's *Pierre*." I correct her and roll my R the same way Papa pronounces my name. Pierre the Skull Hunter.

"I want to dissect a pig next time," Zach says.

"Murderer," Bo groans. Bo turned vegetarian after he watched a documentary about hamburgers.

"It's not murder, it's already *dead*," Tyler says. "Right, Mrs. Dixie? My brother dissected a pig in high school. We don't have to kill the pig, right?"

The girls squeal, and Mrs. Dixie takes a deep breath. "No one kills any animals *ever* in school," she says and clears her throat. "But we're getting off track. Everything we've been learning in Science, and everything we'll be studying for the next six weeks will help prepare us for...?"

Everyone stops fidgeting and stares at Mrs. Dixie, who is being very dramatic about opening her desk drawer. She pulls out a stack of orange papers and hugs them to her.

"Fifth grade—"

"Adventure Camp!" everyone shouts and makes happy noises.

How did this happen so soon? I wonder. We waited and waited and waited, but now that it's happening, I'm sort of surprised. My heart is thunking hard like everyone else, but it's because of another reason. A secret reason.

"Class, today I'm handing out permission packets for the Fifth Grade Adventure Camp. These are very important papers. We're going to Adventure Camp in six weeks, so it's important that your parents turn in the completed packets, including a notarized permission form, by next Tuesday. Next Tuesday. When are you going to turn in your signed and notarized packet?"

"Next Tuesday," everyone sings.

The entire class is squealing about our three-day camping trip. Canoes, campfires, s'mores, nature trails, and ghost stories. Fifth Grade Adventure Camp is legendary.

I take an orange packet from Megan and pass the stack. I stare at the words "Dear Parents," but the rest of the words jumble into a sea of jitters. The other kids' voices tumble together in my head and their excitement swirls down and around in my stomach.

I smile and try to tell myself not to worry. *You'll be fine,* I say in my head. *You hardly ever have accidents at night anymore. You've gone, what, seven whole nights without having an accident?*

But I can feel my secret squirming around, ready to escape if I'm not careful. And in the back of my mind, I hear everyone chanting, "PEE-AIR! PEE-AIR! PEE-AIR!"

CHAPTER 2

The Stinky Chair

FRIDAYS ARE my favorite day of the week. Especially if I've had a "rather successful week," which is Mom's code words for a dry week. I wish my Mom wouldn't say things like that, but she's proud of me, even if it's an embarrassing accomplishment.

But this Friday is like an episode of Good Day/Bad Day. Before lunch, everything is great. Good Day! But the boys and girls go and have an epic fight at recess because of—you guessed it—Keepie Ball. Bad Day! So now everyone is in the land of Not Talking To Each Other, including me, because we wouldn't have had all this mess if we'd only played *my* game. Tag rules, mostly because I'm swift and stealthy.

I use sophisticated words like that because Papa says all the sophisticated words come from France.

I wonder if swift and stealthy are French words?

I've just written Pierre the Swift and Stealthy on my notebook when in walks a new girl. How can I describe her?

She's a quiet girl. And shy. And she's not like the other girls in class. I think she notices me, but I can't be sure. She's very nice to look at, too. She has long blond hair and clear blue eyes. And if I were interested in girls, I might be interested in her. You have to know that I'm not usually interested in girls.

Really.

But Miss Quiet Girl is interesting. (Good Day!)

She stands so still there beside the open doorway that Mrs. Dixie doesn't even notice for a whole minute. Right when I'm about to raise my hand and tell Mrs. Dixie we have company, some of the kids start giggling, which makes Mrs. Dixie do her flat-tire impression: SHHH! She looks up and finds Miss Quiet Girl standing there.

"Come in," Mrs. Dixie says, and waves at Miss Nice To Look At Quiet Girl (do not tell anyone I called her that). "May I help you?"

"I'm new. This is my first day."

She has a quiet voice, too. Like a bird. I can hardly hear her. She is saying something about Georgia and unpacking.

I lean over to the side because Megan's big head is in the way and I can't read Miss Quiet Girl's lips. I lean a little more, a little more. I don't realize that I'm leaning over a little *too* more until it's too late.

Suddenly, my chair is crashing sideways, and I'm eating carpet that tastes like old socks.

"PEE-AIRRR!" Megan and Katelyn wail. Like I've embarrassed them. I really hate whiny girls. (Papa says "hate" is not a good word to describe people, but he doesn't know Megan and Katelyn). By the time I grab my things and sit back in my chair, the whole class is staring at me and shaking their heads like I'm a complete freak.

"Pierre, please control your chair," Mrs. Dixie says, frowning. Then she turns back to the new girl and says, "You're Cynthia Meadows? I think you're supposed to be in Mr. Sullivan's homeroom. Yes. Let me walk you across the hall. Get back to work, students."

What! She's leaving? This is not fair. (Bad, Terrible Day!) I'm not sure why, but I'm really offended by this news. My heart stomps around in my chest and I want to shout "Nooo!" like Luke Skywalker did when he found out who his real father was.

But I don't feel embarrassed anymore about falling out of my chair because you know why? Number one, Miss Nice To Look At Quiet Girl whose name is Cynthia smiled just a tiny bit when I was getting back into my chair. I'm pretty sure she looked at me in the eyes for a second.

And number two, she knows my name.

(Good Day!)

ᖇ◯ᖇ

My entire day yoyos like this. In science class, I nearly fall off my chair again when Mrs. Dixie tells us that we're going to learn physics.

"Physics?" I say, probably too loud because everyone turns around and stares at me. "Real physics?"

I love physics because Albert Einstein was a master of physics, and I want to be like Einstein. If my hair isn't brushed and I stick out my tongue, I already sort of look like him.

Max groans, "Is physics like physical exercise? I can't take another gym class."

"No," I say. "It's like math and science high-fiving each other." At least I think it is. Physics has something to do with matter and energy, which hold the secrets of the universe. At least I think they do. My feet dance around under the table.

In my mind, I'm a Jedi at physics.

But in real life, I keep getting a dumb C on the weekly science pop quiz. Which means I am *not* a Jedi *or* a genius brain *or* Albert Einstein and I will probably *fail* the big physics test.

Papa says don't over-worry, no one's a genius. Papa says that even Einstein had to work and work and work to look like a genius. He says genius is "the accumulation of hard work and lots of failure."

I'm familiar with lots of failure. Look at Three Bright Sides, I tell myself. 1. Bad grades won't make the universe implode. 2. I still love to watch documentaries about space exploration. 3. My brain is very original.

In fifth period, I walk into Mr. Sullivan's math class. Mr. Sullivan is the most amazing teacher. Ever. On the planet. Since the beginning of time.

He's better than your math teacher, guaranteed. He's been teaching for forty years and he can answer ten multiplication facts in three seconds.

If I am Luke Skywalker, he is Yoda Sullivan. He is also not very tall, and he's freakishly wise. On top of that, his classroom is like The Museum of I Want That Stuff. There are so many shelves of stuff, you can't see the walls. Carefully placed on top of the shelves are Lego masterpieces, African masks, collectors' figurines from *Star Wars* and *Raiders of the Lost Ark* and *Star Trek*. He has a model airplane hanging from the ceiling, an autographed poster of Batman, and a real shark curled up in a glass jar of formaldehyde. You would think it's hard to concentrate on math lessons when you're surrounded by a thousand stare-able things.

But no. Mr. Sullivan's Yoda-finger keeps us on track.

I'm hoping just a little that I'll find Cynthia here with the thousand other stare-able things. But no. What I see is Katelyn stooping over her chair, smelling it.

"Gross. I'm not sitting there," she says, fluttering her hand across her nose. Mr. Sullivan isn't in the classroom, so Katelyn puts her hands on her hips and wrinkles her nose. "It smells like poo. I can't sit here!"

"Let's switch it," Megan says. Megan and Katelyn have matching brown ponytails with polka dot ribbons. They're not even sisters.

Before I can sit down, Megan and Katelyn grab my chair and switch it with the stinky chair. Katelyn sits down fast and curls her ankles around the chair legs.

"Hey!" I say. "You can't do that."

"We just did," Megan says. "Besides, there's not a *rule* that says you can't switch chairs. Is there?"

"Big deal," I say, and give them a snarly face. They just laugh. I am not very intimidating.

"Oh, man," Max says. "It does smell like poo. Who sat there last period?"

Everyone shrugs, and I lean over to take a whiff.

I wish I hadn't.

"Quick, Rosemary's chair!" Max whispers.

Max and I shove the stinky chair over to Rosemary's desk. Max slips her chair out and slides it back to my desk, just as Rosemary and Mr. Sullivan walk into the room.

I feel a little guilty. But mostly I'm relieved. I mean, would *you* want to sit in a poo-chair?

By recess, everyone's talking about the stinky chair and trying to figure out who it belongs to. I'm standing in line for dumb kickball because no one wants to play tag. At least we're not playing Keepie-Ball.

"Bo, you're in Mr. Sullivan's homeroom," Max says. "Who sits in that chair?"

"I told you, I don't know. I don't pay attention to that stuff." Bo pushes up his glasses and shakes his ankles. "I'm up next. I'm gonna kick that ball all the way to the kindergarten swings."

"It's someone on the back row," I say. "Who's on the back row?"

"Are you talking about the stinky chair?" Katelyn asks behind me.

"None of your beeswax," I say. But Max suddenly turns into Mr. Charming and smiles at her.

"It's okay, Pierre. Maybe she can help." Then Max sort of freezes with that goofy smile on his face.

Katelyn smiles, too.

"Help?" I ask. "Did you forget? She tried to sabotage my chair."

"Well, *you* sabotaged Rosemary's chair," Katelyn says.

That's when I notice Rosemary standing in line behind Katelyn. Rosemary has her arms crossed and her lips smashed in a frown.

"My dress smells like potty now. Smell it!"

She pulls the back of her dress to the front, and everyone backs away squealing "NO!"

"I smell like the restroom on Burrito Thursdays, Pee-Air!" Rosemary shouts.

"Hey, I'm sorry," I say. "I didn't think it would rub off on your clothes." But inside my head, I'm thinking, *Whew! That could have been my jeans.* And how did I get blamed for this? I point to Katelyn.

"Katelyn started it. She should be apologizing to me."

"I'm sorry," Katelyn says to me with her nose in the air. "But I'm not really sorry. You'd do the same to me if I wasn't there first."

"No I wouldn't."

"Yes you would."

"No I wouldn't."

"Liar."

"No I'm not."

"Who *cares*?" Bo says. "You're breaking my concentration!"

"FYI, Bo," Katelyn says, "you're not going to kick the ball to the kindergarten swings." She turns to me and squints her blue eyes. "And FYI, we'll see if you're telling the truth next week."

"What?" I say. "That doesn't even make sense. I don't think you know what FYI means."

"Yes I do. For Your Information."

"It still doesn't make sense."

Max interrupts. "She's saying that you're a liar if you give her the stinky chair next week. Because you said you wouldn't." He smiles at Katelyn again and then pats me on the shoulder. "Sorry, buddy."

They all stand there staring at me while the whole thing sinks in. I've trapped myself. If Katelyn switches her stinky chair with mine, I can't switch it back, unless I want to be called a liar.

"Max! Meeting!" I say, pulling him out of the line.

"But I'm up after Bo!" he says.

"Forget kickball. What am I going to do? She's going to give me the stinky chair tomorrow."

"Yeah. That stinks." Max smiles. Then he laughs and slugs my arm. "Get it? It stinks!"

"Yeah. It's not funny."

"Don't worry. We'll just switch chairs with someone else."

"But Katelyn will call me a liar."

"Who cares?"

"I do."

"Do you want to smell like poo every day?" he asks.

"No." Not poo, not pee, not anything.

"Then it's every man for himself. But don't worry. I'll help you."

CHAPTER 3

The Worst Feeling in the World

Over the weekend, Max helps me brainstorm ways to avoid the stinky chair, and we finally land on a foolproof way. Get to class early like a stealthy Jedi and make sure my chair doesn't smell. Simple! On Monday, I run-walk to math class to get there early to execute my secret plan. But nearly everyone else is already there. It seems my secret plan isn't so secret. All the kids are leaning over their chairs, sniffing them.

"*What* is going on?" Mr. Sullivan says as he walks in the room.

Everyone sits down quickly and pretends like nothing's wrong. If we're very good and very quiet, Mr. Sullivan will tell us stories about fascinating events in his life, like the time he jumped out of an airplane with only a parachute and a brand new camera, which he dropped about three seconds after he exited the plane. (The camera, not the parachute.)

Sometimes Mr. Sullivan's stories go on so long, I wonder if we'll have time for math. And for the record, I'm okay with that. But he always manages to surprise us, and right when you least expect it, he snaps out of his fantastic memory and says something like, "All right! Time for Factor Trees!"

But today I'm not thinking about Sulli-stories. I'm thinking about my seat.

Katelyn raises her eyebrows and smirks at me. *Pure evil, that smile is,* my Jedi-brain tells me. She must have given me the stinky chair.

Please please please, I think. *Don't let it be me.*

I drop my pencil in a smooth maneuver to smell the chair seat. I'm not sure if my seat stinks or not. I sniff again.

"Mr. François!" Mr. Sullivan says. "Are you having a problem you'd like to share with us?"

I sit up like a snapped rubber band. "No, sir."

"Good."

My heart is pounding so hard, I can't think. Normally, my ears are on high alert because nobody, especially me, would want to disappoint the legendary Mr. Sullivan. But I have no idea what Mr. Sullivan is saying for the next half hour because I'm too busy taking deep breaths to figure out if my chair stinks, and all those deep breaths just make me dizzy. It's not until the end of class that I notice a sick expression on Zach's face. He turns around and gives Katelyn a scowl. Then he lifts his bottom and sits on his foot.

"Bingo!" Max whispers. "Pierre! Zach got the Stinky Chair."

Zach says to me under his breath, "This means war, Francy-pants."

For a whole week, math class is like musical chairs, except instead of the usual routine, the Stinky Chair is sliding around the room like a bobsled to the tune of "Hurry Before Mr. Sullivan Walks In." By sheer luck, I haven't gotten the stinky chair yet. But it's only a matter of time. I have nightmares about it.

That's all I need: someone to accuse me of cutting the cheese right in the middle of math class. Papa says that in France, cutting the cheese is a privilege. French cheese is stinky, but at least it tastes good. *Nothing* tastes good about cutting the cheese in America.

When Max and Bo and I walk home, I can't stop thinking about the Stinky Chair.

Max and Bo nearly clobber me with the football. The ball whooshes past my head and grazes my ear.

"Hey!" I yell.

"Sorry," Bo says. "Wake up, Sleeping Beauty. You're supposed to catch the ball."

"I was thinking."

"Not about that dumb chair again," Max says, and shakes his head at Bo. "He's obsessed."

"I'm not either." I try to think of something else, but I can't help myself. "Hey, Bo. Did you figure out who sits at the desk beside mine in Mr. Sullivan's homeroom?"

"Jeez! What am I? A detective?" Bo says. He tosses the ball in a high, perfect spiral and then catches it.

"All you had to do was look," I say.

"I'm just kidding. Everyone knows who sits in the Stinky Chair."

"Who?" Max and I say together.

"Mason Higgins. Who else?"

Mason Higgins is the meanest kid in fifth grade. His clothes are always wrinkled and stained, and you *would* feel sorry for him because maybe he's poor or his mother doesn't care enough to wash his clothes...but you can't feel sorry because he cusses *All. The. Time.*

"Mason Higgins," Max repeats.

"Makes sense," I add. "It figures. I don't know who's worse: Mason or Katelyn."

"Why Katelyn?" Max asks.

"What? Because she's the one who started the chair-switching every day!" I say.

"I'm not worried. You know why I'm not worried?" Max asks me. He tosses the football back to Bo and misses by a mile. "Because I'm nice to Katelyn. You see the way I smile at her? Girls like to be smiled at."

"I smile."

"Not *at* her."

"I don't think smiling will help. She doesn't even like me. I don't know why."

"Girl-charm. It's your best defense. Hey, did you get your Adventure Camp papers turned in?"

"Not yet."

"You better hurry. The deadline is Tuesday, right? Hey, I'll see you tomorrow." He waves at Bo and me as we all part ways at the stop sign.

I spend the rest of the walk home trying to figure out a foolproof way to avoid getting the Stinky Chair. Maybe I can hide in the bathroom. Maybe I should buy rubber pants. Maybe I could borrow a wheelchair and pretend I've broken both legs. You see? I lack problem-solving skills. So I practice smiling and girl-charms instead.

At dinner, I want to talk to Mom and Papa about those Adventure Camp papers, but I'm nervous. I know we'll end up talking about bathroom stuff and "rather successful weeks," and unfortunately, this week wasn't one of them. So I tell Mom about the latest Sulli-stories instead.

"Ages and ages ago," I start as Dad takes off his chef's apron, "Mr. Sullivan played baseball in high school. Once, when he reached too high up to catch a fly ball, he flipped backward over the outfield fence, and landed on his feet with the ball *In. His. Mitt*! We all clapped so loud, Mrs. Angler stuck her head in the room and gave us the stink-eye."

"That's nice, sweetie," Mom says. "Shall we eat?"

"Sure." I wait for Mom to take the first bite because that's what proper French boys do. And because Papa makes me. "But today, Mr. Sullivan told us the best story of all. Mr. Sullivan's college buddy became a teacher, too. But poor Denny. He made bad choices, and became addicted to drugs. After a normal day at school, Denny transformed into a *desperate criminal of the night*."

It's such a great story, I'm careful to include all the details. "He used his entire paycheck to buy drugs. Then he sold all his furniture to buy more drugs. And when everything was gone but the kitchen table, he went out and robbed houses to get even more money for drugs. And then he'd wake up the next morning and teach third graders."

Mom stops chewing her food and raises her eyebrows. "Is that an appropriate story to tell fifth graders?" she asks Papa.

"Wait. It gets worse!" I say. "Then Denny accidentally shot and *killed* an old man he was robbing. Now he's in jail for the rest of his life. A life wasted because of drugs."

Mom chokes on her dinner roll. Papa says Mr. Sullivan is *unconventional*. I don't tell them that Mr. Sullivan had tears in his eyes when he finished the story of his old buddy Denny. The whole classroom was silent as he blew his nose on a tissue and turned on the projector. I listened to my heart pounding and swore I would never, ever do drugs, because watching Mr. Sullivan's eyes all watery was almost more than I could handle.

At dessert, I finally get around to the Adventure Camp papers, which have been sitting on the kitchen counter for over a week.

"The deadline is tomorrow. Why haven't you signed them yet?"

"Well, actually, I'm having doubts about whether you should go," she says, then glances at Papa.

"I have to. *Everyone's* going."

"You don't *have* to, you know," Papa says.

I think about Bo and Max in a rustic cabin with lanterns and ghost stories and marshmallow treats. When they're not fighting, they'll be having the best time of their lives. I can't miss that, even if I'm worried about the nights.

Mom stacks up the empty plates on the table. "The problem is one of those papers we have to sign says that they're not responsible for any accidents that might happen. So, if you broke your arm because—I don't know—the bunk beds are rotten, they can legally say it's not their fault."

"I promise I won't sleep in a rotten bunk bed."

"What if you catch pneumonia from hiking in the cold? It's been a cold October."

"I'll wear a coat and hat and gloves. I won't catch pneumonia, right Papa?"

He takes a sip of wine and nods at Mom. "We can't be certain, but statistically speaking, it's unlikely that Pierre will get pneumonia."

"And what about...other kinds of accidents?" Mom takes a drink and sloshes the water around in her glass.

I shrug. "I'm not worried." Not *too* worried, I think.

"You're not worried?"

"Nope." I give her my best not-worried smile.

"Are *you* worried?" she asks Papa.

He takes another sip of wine and shrugs. "What is the worst that could happen?"

I could wet all my extra underwear. I'd have to wear Biggies diapers. Everyone would find out I still have accidents. I could drown the whole cabin in pee, and we'd only be rescued by firemen through a hole in the roof.

My super-brain has an idea. "Maybe you can volunteer to be a cabin-dad," I say. It's a genius plan!

"Oh, no. No no no."

I give him my best Pierre the Sad-Eye look.

"No," Papa laughs. "I'm allergic to camping. You're on your own."

I *will* be on my own. Mom won't be there to make sure I look like a normal kid with a normal body. I was doing really well until a few nights ago. Then whammy. I woke up in Lake Doom. Every time I think I'm cured of accidents, I wake up and discover that I'm cursed again.

It's the worst feeling in the world.

The doctor says I was born with a small bladder. We've tried all kinds of things to cure me. No water after dinner. No water *with* dinner. Alarms that hook onto my underwear and go off like sirens in the middle of the night. Little prescription pills.

Nothing cured me. The doctor said not to worry. That I would most likely grow out of accidents by the time I was ten.

I'm ten now. Mom and Papa act like it's no big deal, but I think deep inside we're all officially worried.

I look at Papa and Mom and Papa again, and push down the baguette ball in my throat. I'm waiting for them to bring up Biggies—those "big-boy diapers" that I've refused to wear since I was eight. *Don't bring up the Biggies*, I think. *Don't say it!*

They don't. But suddenly I realize that if I have an accident, not only will I have to sneak to the bathroom to change my pajamas without a dozen kids noticing, but Mom won't be there to change my sheets and make the curse disappear.

Of course my brain's not completely on board about going to camp, but I've been waiting to go to Adventure Camp since I was five years old.

"Please, mom?" I clasp my hands together and give Mom my best pleading eyes. "I don't want to be the only kid left behind. I'll have to stay with the fourth graders and do boring worksheets."

"Well, okay," she finally says. "But if you fall off a cliff or get pneumonia, I'm suing the camp *and* the school anyway."

"Fine with me!" And I *am* fine. I feel like dancing around the kitchen, but Papa would say that's not good French manners.

"So, what's pneumonia exactly?" I ask.

Mom shakes her head and smiles.

"Pierre," Papa says, "you're sure you want to go?"

I nod my head and chew on a baguette. I am a little worried.

"Two nights in a cabin? Away from your own bed? We'll be hours away, you know."

"I'll be fine," I say, and convince my mouth to smile. "No problem."

But I know that no one at the table believes me.

CHAPTER 4

The Spelling Bee

I KNOW I am not your average kid. It's not because I'm half-French.

Or maybe it is.

There was that time in Paris when Papa taught me my first sentence in French: *"Je parle français comme une vache espagnole!"* That means, "I speak French like a Spanish cow." I practiced it over and over, because it's hilarious, right? I couldn't wait to talk to the other French kids on the playground.

I thought it was a great way to meet people. Evidently, they didn't.

Average ten-year-olds don't prefer vegetables over pizza. Average ten-year-olds in Texas don't beg to watch BBC documentaries on nature and the universe instead of football.

(Watching football is cruel and unusual punishment, but *Don't. Tell. Anyone.*)

Average ten-year-olds don't call their classmates "acquaintances" and use the word "evidently" as much as possible. I love that word "evidently." I saw it in *Calvin & Hobbes* (the greatest cartoon since...cartoons) and decided I needed to use it.

Evidently, I'm succeeding.

That's why when it comes to contests and grades, I really really really really want to win. If I'm not average, then I must be a winner. Because if I'm not a winner, and I'm not average, then maybe I'm just weird. For the record, I'm okay with that. But when you're in an entire grade of mean fifth-graders, being That Grand-Prize Winner is better than being That Weird Francy-pants.

So every time I stopped at the water fountain this week and saw the poster about the Spelling Bee, a bolt of I've-Gotta-Win-That-Thing shivered down my spine.

Today is the day.

Mrs. Dixie starts class with a big smile on her face. "It's about time for the Morton Elementary Spelling Bee. All the grade-levels are participating at the same time. In five minutes, we're going to line up and join the other fifth graders."

Her announcement sends a current of excitement through the classroom. Papers are shuffling and kids are wiggling in their seats. We sound like a herd of starving piglets. We can't help it. Spelling Bees are like nature documentaries. Survival of the Fittest.

In my head, I win. In my head, I'm what people call a Dark Horse.

A Dark Horse is a winner that comes out of nowhere and *ka-zam*! Trophy time. I've got a wreath of roses around my neck! I swish my tail and stomp my hooves in victory!

Reality is often different from what goes on in my head.

With seventy-three fifth graders lined up in the cafeteria, my body's been tricked. It thinks I'm here for lunch, so I'm nervous *and* hungry. Hannah is the first on the stage.

"Hannah Azel, your word is *banana*," Mrs. Dixie begins.

"Can you repeat the word?" Hannah asks.

"*Banana*."

"Can you use it in a sentence?"

Mrs. Dixie sighs. "Okay. I can't hear you—I have a banana in my ear."

Hannah says again, nearly shouting, "I *said*, can you use it in a sentence?"

That Hannah cracks me up. But I'm not laughing about fifteen minutes later. The words started out first-grade-easy, and almost all seventy-three of us got through the first round. Now that it's the second round, kids are dropping like flies. All the boys except me have been disqualified, and I'm the only boy standing with nine girls in front of the entire fifth grade.

The new girl Cynthia is one of the nine girls, and I can't stop looking at her.

Part of me is like, "Hooray! I'm the only boy left!" The other part is like, "Oh no. I'm the only boy left."

The pressure is crushing.

"Pierre! Pierre!" the boys chant when it's my turn. Even the ones who call me Francy-Pants are stomping their feet for me.

"Quiet!" Mrs. Angler shouts from the side of the cafeteria. I'm pretty sure she's rooting for the girls.

Mrs. Dixie reads from her list. Every teacher in the United States has to read the same list of words in the exact same order. It's fair that way. Except that some kids get words like "professional" and "acceptable" and the next kid gets the word "baby."

"Pierre, your word is *evidently*."

Yes! "Evidently," I repeat. I use that word all the time. Then I realize that saying it and spelling it are two different things. I squeeze my eyes shut, imagine I'm sprawled out on the floor staring at my *Calvin & Hobbes* collection, and I go for it.

"E-v-i-d-e-n-t-l-y." I open my eyes.

All the boys are holding their breath and staring at Mrs. Dixie, too.

"That is correct," she announces. The whole cafeteria erupts into cheers, and the boys jump up and give high fives.

"Quiet, boys!" Mr. Sullivan shouts this time. "Sit down, or no stories at math!"

That shuts everyone up. I'm feeling pretty good. I even smile at Katelyn when she's up, and say "good job!" when she gets hers right. Maybe fifth graders aren't so bad after all.

The victory doesn't last long. Mrs. Dixie starts reading words I've never even heard of: egregious, defiance, demure. And the girls just keep getting them right.

Girls must have a special spelling gene in their DNA.

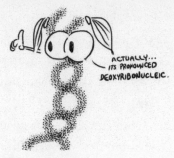

ACTUALLY...
ITS PRONOUNCED
DEOXYRIBONUCLEIC.

They zip through the round, and suddenly it's my turn again.

"Pierre, your word is *antipathy*."

"Ant-whatie?"

"Antipathy."

She reads the word in a sentence, but it doesn't help. I have no idea what this word means or looks like. The boys are holding their breath and leaning toward the stage. Max and Bo fall off their seats and scramble back before Mr. Sullivan yells at them.

I close my eyes again and start. "A-n-t-i-p-a-t-y."

"I'm sorry. That is incorrect," Mrs. Dixie says.

The girl behind me spells the word the exact same way I did. Except she remembers the "h."

"How could you forget the 'h'? That's the easiest part, dude," Zach says after the Spelling Bee is over.

"I know," I say. "That was dumb."

I've been avoiding Zach since he promised revenge in the Stinky Chair wars. But here he is with all of the other boys, crowding around me and giving me handshakes.

"It's okay." Zach pats my shoulder. "You got farther than any of us. Good job."

If there's one thing that I'm learning about life from fifth grade, it's that humans are not good or bad. They're both. They're like Dr. Jekyll and Mr. Hyde. If you're not familiar with the story,

Jekyll is your normal, everyday mad scientist during the day—a nice guy who likes to experiment in his lab. But at night he turns into Mr. Hyde, a monster who terrorizes the city.

We have a lot of Jekyll/Hydes in our school. Sometimes she's a teacher, who bakes cookies for the whole class one day.

The next day, she cancels recess for the entire class and gives everyone a pop quiz instead.

Sometimes Jekyll/Hyde is a student. Like Megan. "May I borrow a pencil, Pierre?" in the morning. "STOP TOUCHING MY DESK, PEE-AIR!" in the afternoon.

There is one person who may be the only person in Morton Elementary who doesn't have a Hyde inside. You Know Who. Maybe that's why I don't even mind when I lose and she wins first place at the Spelling Bee.

⊙⊂⊃⊙

"How did the Spelling Bee go?" Mom asks after school.

"B-a-d. I didn't win."

"Well, winning's not everything, right?"

"Mom, winning is kind of the whole point of Spelling Bees. But it's okay. The new girl won. So I don't mind."

"Who's the new girl?" Mom stops hunting for her fancy coat and looks at me.

I don't know why, but it's hard to say Cynthia's name out loud. "Just a girl," I say. Actually, Mom is the perfect person to ask about girls. She's practically a girl herself.

"Mom," I say as casually as I can, "how do you get someone to like you?"

"Just be yourself. You're a nice person. Who wouldn't like you?"

I decide to tell her everything. The true confessions of Pierre François. "I have to tell you something, a secret. But you have to promise not to laugh."

"Okay. I promise."

"No, really. You have to promise not to laugh."

"I won't laugh. I promise."

"All right," I sigh. "I officially have my first crush. It's the new girl. I can't stop looking at her."

Mom smiles.

"You promised not to laugh!"

"I'm not laughing," she says, but then her smile gets so big I can see all her teeth. "I'm sorry. It's just nice, that's all. So tell me about her."

"There's not much to tell. She's nice. And quiet. It's *so* nice that she's quiet."

Mom gives me a strange look. "Really? You know, there's nothing wrong with girls having a strong voice. For a long time, girls weren't even allowed to go to school. So it's a good thing that girls feel comfortable, after hundreds of years of oppression, to express themselves–"

"No, Mom," I interrupt her lecture. "I mean she doesn't scream in class and she's not rude like all the other girls."

"Oh. Well, rude isn't good."

"This girl isn't rude."

"You mean the new girl?"

"Yeah, her. So, um. How do you get a crush to notice you? Should I tell her she's my crush? I want to tell her. But I don't want to tell her. But I think I want her to know. What should I do?"

Mom pulls a fuzzy coat out and closes the closet. "Have you told Bo or Max? Maybe they can drop her a hint. That's the way we used to do it, anyway."

"What? No way! This is super confidential, Mom. No one in fifth grade can keep a secret." It's true. Hunter told everyone that Tyler watched the Barbie Dreams Movie, and Tyler told everyone that Diego once ate a piece of dog food.

"I just want *her* to know. What should I do?"

I follow Mom into her bedroom. Papa's in there, dressed in a fancy suit and tie. He's slipping on his shiny black shoes for the opera.

"What should you do about what?" Papa asks.

"Nothing," I say.

Mom opens her closet. "Pierre has a crush, and he's asking for advice. What dress should I wear? The long black one?"

"Mom!" I say, "It's supposed to be a secret."

"Don't worry," Papa says. "I won't tell a soul. I know nothing about crushes. I know nothing about women."

"What about Mom?"

"I stand corrected. I only know about one woman in the whole world. Your mom. The only woman who would have me. Right, Mom?"

"Mm-hmm," she mumbles and tosses her dress on the bed. "Pierre, I have to get ready for the opera. Just...be yourself with your crush. Say hello, and if she doesn't notice you, that's her loss."

"But what happens after I say hello? What do I talk to her about?" We could get stuck there for eternity saying hello to each other, because who knows what comes next?

"Honey, we're going to be late."

"Okay."

"And pack your overnight bag. You're staying with Max tonight."

"Woo-hoo!" I jump up. "The whole night?"

"Is that okay?"

"Sure!" I race to my room and throw my clothes and toothbrush into my bag. It's only the second time I've spent the night at Max's, and I don't even need my pajamas because we stay up all night eating Cheesy Puffs and beating our high scores on MarioKart. What's there to worry about?

CHAPTER 5

Inappropriate Language

MAX HAS FIVE brothers and sisters, so spending a night at his house is a *special event*. Max hardly ever invites anyone over, probably because his mom's already overrun by kids. And when I ring the doorbell, I'm half-holding my breath that she doesn't change her mind.

"What's one more?" his mother says to mine when we walk in. "Have fun at the opera. And if you can't find him when you get back, we'll just give you one of ours."

"Ha ha," the twins say. They elbow their way beside me as we walk down the hallway to Max's room.

"Bye, Mom!" I holler before she can pull me back to have a private *tête-a-tête* about tonight. I packed a pair of sweatpants and a towel to sleep on, just in case, but I do *not* want to have a conversation about it.

"Okay...have fun!" I hear her say nervously.

"Give us some space!" Max says to all the kids that have crowded around me. His brothers and sisters are younger than Max, and they're all touching me like I'm Jesus or something.

"You can't make us leave," the twins Luke and Larson say, as if they've rehearsed it. "It's our room, too."

Luke and Larson are nine, and one year behind us in Morton Elementary. They're okay so far. They haven't been body-snatched by aliens or anything yet.

The rest of the night we spend playing video games and building war worlds out of Legos.

Max's mother sticks her head in our room and says, "Max, it's eleven-thirty!"

"Can we stay up? We're not even tired," Max says. He looks at me. "Right, Pierre?"

"Right."

"And we just started building this Minecraft fort to protect us from zombies."

Max's mother looks at Luke and Larson, who are passed out on the top bunk bed. "Okay. But don't wake up your brothers or sisters. Or me or your dad. So keep it quiet, Mister, or you're in big trouble."

"Okay." Max grins and gives me a high five.

"Goodnight, sweet Pierre. I know you'll be quiet." Max's mother winks at me and closes the door.

"Goodnight, sweet Pierre," Max says in a high, girlie voice. "I know *you'll* be quiet. You're my sweet sugar bumpkins."

"Shush up," I say. "I can't help it that I'm naturally sweet. It's my French DNA."

My plan is to make a Lego masterpiece and take a photograph of it for the Lego website, and then to play video games until sunrise. No sleep for me! We pull out the extra bed mat and layer it with blankets so it's nice and soft, even though I'm not planning on going to the Dreamland of Railroads and Other Perfect Places to Pee. At about one in the morning, Max falls over onto his pillow with the game controller still in his hand.

The last thing I remember is sprouting wings and flying through space.

Don't fall asleep, my brain shouts. But it's too late. Suddenly, I'm staring at a Max's clock flashing 4:00 AM and my heart is racing.

It's still dark outside, and Max and his brothers are all snoring in their beds. Somehow, I've ended up under the blankets and I'm sweating like a football player.

At least I think it's sweat.

I press my hand on the damp sheet beneath me. Holy crapola.

It's not sweat. It's *accident*. My heart starts pumping double-time. I get up as quietly as I can, grab my overnight bag, and sneak to the bathroom. The light bulb in there is like a big fat pointing finger of Look What You Did, so I turn it off and change clothes in the dark. I stuff the wet pants at the bottom of my bag and put on my clean sweatpants.

I stoop over my bellybutton and snarl at my bladder. "Why can't you just grow some muscles! Jeez!"

The bigger problem is figuring out how to hide the evidence: a stinky bed sheet and blanket. I'd have to stuff them in the washing machine, wherever *that* is, before anyone wakes up.

Once my eyes adjust to the dark, I'm a little more confident that I can complete the mission. My imagination helps at times like these:

I'm a spy. A spy with a dark, terrible secret. I lug the sheets that hold...what? I know! These sheets hold the bound body of CIA's Most Wanted: Mr. Diggs. How was I to know that my own dog was a double-spy? And now I must deliver him to Headquarters. I press my back against the wall and inch down the hallway with my hand drawn up like a pistol.

The washing machine isn't that hard to find, after all. I toss Mr. Diggs into the washer tub, give him a salute, and sneak back to Max's room without disturbing anyone.

I've still got two dry blankets left. So I crawl between the layers and stare at the deep-sea-blue ceiling. That was a rather successful solution to a rather unsuccessful night, I tell myself. Thanks to my genius-brain.

See? It's nothing you couldn't take care of. You're fine!

I try to close my eyes, but all I can see is a swinging Adventure Camp sign, a cabin with a dozen kids, a long night, and not a washing machine in sight.

e◯e

When Mom picks me up the next morning, I've almost forgotten about the accident. Which I prefer. After all, if you can't control something, it's best to think about Minecraft instead. That's my motto, anyway.

But Mom is concerned about my *physical well-being*. "Did you have a good night? You know, a comfortable one?"

"Yeah," I say.

"A dry one?" she adds.

"Not exactly. But don't worry, Mom. I took care of it. I found the machine and put the bed stuff in, and no one even knew."

"Oh." She nods and stares at the road. "Did you check to see if the machine was empty before you put in the wet sheets?"

"What do you mean empty?" I say.

"Never mind. I'm proud of you, sweetheart." She smiles at me. "You know, it's not your fault that you have accidents."

"I know," I say. "It's my stupid bladder. My dumb, retarded bladder."

"Pierre, don't say those words."

"What words?"

"Any of them. But especially the R-word. It's not appropriate language."

I wonder how Mom would react to hearing Mason Higgins cuss. She'd probably call the principal. And then Mason Higgins would sit on me at recess.

"Stupid is not that bad, considering the other words I hear kids say at school."

"That may be true. But you know what Papa says about inappropriate language."

When we pull into the garage, I'm trying to remember what Papa says about Inappropriate Language. Then we walk into the kitchen and Papa gives me a free lecture about taboos and lexicons and euphemisms and other big words that make my eyes droopy and my brain groggy.

Some time later, I wake up drooling on the kitchen table, and Papa and Mama are debating about word origins and other things that put me to sleep in the first place.

"Papa," I say, wiping the sleep out of my eyes. "If I can't call my bladder stupid or dumb or the r-word—"

"Or any other euphemism."

"Yeah, that. Then what can I call it?"

"How about 'expletive'?"

"Expa-whatie?"

"An expletive is any sort of foul language. So just say expletive instead of the curse word."

"You want me to say expletive?" I say, not quite sure how to use it.

"Honey, I think he'll get in trouble at school," Mom says.

"Nonsense," Papa laughs. "Give it a go, Pierre. *That expletive bladder*! Now there's an insult."

"That expletive bladder," I say.

"Say it with conviction!" Papa says.

I take a deep breath and shout, "That expletive bladder!" It doesn't quite deliver the punch, but I guess it will do.

"I almost forgot!" Mom says, "I bought you those jeans you were asking for." She tosses me a store bag that crunches as it lands in my arms.

Some boys like fancy athletic shoes. I prefer cool pants with fancy zippers.

"The Lucky Jeans? With the zippers on the sides?" I pull the jeans out and place them against my legs. They hang down to my shoes, and the brass zippers are perfect for secret things I need to stash. Suddenly, my whole day feels lucky. I imagine wearing them to school and getting a 100 on my science quiz.

"I hope you like them. They cost a fortune."

"I love them. Thanks, Mom."

I wear them all weekend and won't take them off until Sunday night for Mom to wash. I don't even worry about accidents or school because what's to worry about when you have Lucky Jeans with brass zippers?

CHAPTER 6

The Luckiest Day

MY LUCKY JEANS aren't lucky jeans.

First, I forget my lunchbox in the back seat of Mom's car. And today is Meat Surprise day in the cafeteria. Ugh. Second, my vocabulary homework isn't in my folder, so Mrs. Dixie signs my planner. Third, I finally get enough people to play tag at AM recess, but no one will chase me because I'm so fast. Eventually, even Bo and Max abandon me for Keepie Ball.

Just when I think it can't get any worse, I'm late to math class. Well, not late-late, but I arrive right as Mr. Sullivan is walking back into the room. That's too late. I'm just about to sit down in my chair and whip out my math spiral, but in the corner of my eye, I see Katelyn staring at me.

Then I see Zach. He's turned all the way around in his seat, waiting for me to sit down. He has crazy-face.

I think I have radar senses, because it feels like a million alarms start ringing my head. Eee-awww! Eee-awww! Eee-awww! Then I notice Max's eyes, all white and wide, and his eyebrows hiked up to his hairline.

So I quick-bend-over and sniff and *Oh. My. Snog.*

I've got the Stinky Chair.

It smells like toenails and belly buttons. I hold my hand against my clamped mouth so I don't lose my lunch.

Katelyn is staring at the whiteboard like an innocent bystander. She finally did it.

"Pierre got it," I hear someone whisper.

"Expletive!" I whisper. It's the first word that comes to mind, and it isn't quite satisfying. Max shrugs at me and faces the front, where Mr. Sullivan is erasing the whiteboard.

"Settle down everyone and get out your homework," he says.

And to think of all those times I smiled at her! Wasted smiles!

I lower my butt down slowly, slowly. So slowly that my butt never quite makes it to the seat. Maybe I can just stay like this during math class, frozen in a chair-like position.

Mr. Sullivan draws some shapes on the board and talks about polygons and quadrilaterals. I'm taking notes, and thinking this dreaded situation isn't so bad. I'm a genius. But after a minute, my thighs start getting warm. Then they're shaking. And burning.

"I want you to copy all of these figures on the board," Mr. Sullivan says as he fills the board with shapes.

Suddenly, a brilliant plan pops into my head. Just when my shaky legs are begging for mercy, I quietly shove one of the Stinky Chair legs backward with my foot and slowly dip down down down until I'm kneeling on the carpet behind my desk.

Mr. Sullivan still hasn't turned around long enough to notice that I'm not actually sitting in my chair. So I stretch up my torso and hunch over my desk. I don't even need a chair!

It's the most brilliant plan I've ever improvised.

Einstein would be proud of me.

Being on the back row has its advantages. So does having a genius brain.

I don't even get into trouble. Hunter Longstreet does.

"Mr. Longstreet," Mr. Sullivan says. "I saw what you did. That was gross. One doesn't wipe one's boogers on one's neighbor's desk."

"Ooooooh," the whole class sings in disgust.

"Go to the Focus Chair."

Hunter Longstreet spends a lot of time in the Focus Chair. He huffs, throws his pencil on the floor, and stomps to the front of the room. He is another not-nice person in fifth grade.

I'm feeling pretty good about avoiding the Stinky Chair disaster when Mr. Sullivan makes an announcement. "Let's play a game. Let's all close our eyes. I'll draw three shapes on the board, and when I say 'Open,' you'll tell me the total perimeter of the shapes I've drawn. The first person with the correct answer will get a point. And the person with the most points will win a Sulli-Photo."

Sulli-Photos are photographs that Mr. Sullivan took on his vacations to London and New York and Hawaii. He turns them into little trading cards, and they are the best photos ever. I've already won two Sulli-Photos from the prize box. Everyone knows which ones I pick because Paris is way better than anywhere.

"Move over, Francy-pants," Katelyn whispers to me. "This Sulli-Photo is mine. And I'm choosing the Statue of Liberty. "

Everyone in class closes their eyes. Everyone except me. Even Mr. Sullivan closes his eyes before he turns around at the board. My brain has another surge of inspiration. It's like Christmas in my brain.

While everyone has their eyes closed, I switch the Stinky Chair with Hunter's. After all, he's not sitting there anymore.

I make it back to my desk and sit in my new chair just as Mr. Sullivan turns around. "Wait!" he calls out.

I freeze. My heart stops.

"I forgot something," Mr. Sullivan says. "Close your eyes again."

My heart bursts into a thousand little beats.

I'm safe! My lucky jeans are safe! I feel a little guilty when Hunter is excused from the Focus Chair and plops down hard on the Stinky Chair seat. But mostly I'm relieved.

I don't win a Sulli-photo, but today I don't care. I'm so happy, I sign my daily work "Pierre the Genius Brain."

At recess, I'm standing in line for dumb kickball again, when I hear Hunter laughing behind me.

"Pee-air got the pee-chair!" he sings. "Pee-air got the pee-chair! Get it? It rhymes." He starts rapping right there, making *pa-choo pa-choo* sounds.

Normally, I'd be so embarrassed by Hunter's mean song, I'd want to melt into a puddle of mud. But today, I just feel sorry for Booger Boy.

A couple of girls cover their mouths and giggle. That's when I notice my secret crush standing there with a surprised expression on her face. Just the rare sight of Cynthia so close to me makes my brain kick into high gear again.

"*You* switched my chair?" I ask Hunter.

He stops rapping and laughs. "Yeah, before class!"

"Well, it didn't work. I actually *didn't* get the Stinky Chair."

"Yeah, right. I saw you sitting in it."

I stick out my derriere. "Want to smell?"

"Gross!" the girls laugh.

"No way," Hunter says. I can see that he's a little confused at my confidence. I'm not normally confident when people say mean things.

"Go ahead," I say, wiggling my bottom and smiling. "It smells like flowers and teddy bears."

Then everyone around me laughs at my funny line. Even Cynthia.

And just like that, today is the luckiest day ever.

CHAPTER 7

A Lot of Hoopla

IT IS ONE week before Adventure Camp, and I'm not scared.

What I am is nervous.

I'm not just talking about a wet-sleeping-bag nightmare. What if there are scorpions in the cabins? What if my canoe tips over onto a nest of baby water moccasins?

"Water moccasins don't live in nests," Bo says at lunch. "You're supposed to be the smart one."

"A nest, a swarm—who cares what you call it when they're eating you for lunch?" I'm not hungry anymore.

Max crushes his juice box. "I don't know. I don't think they allow poisonous snakes in the lake."

"They don't," Bo says, "or my sister would have told me. She went to Adventure Camp, and nobody got bit. They swam in the lake and everything."

"You think we'll get to swim in the lake?" Max asks.

"Are you kidding? It's freezing outside."

"It's not freezing," I say.

"Well, it *will* be freezing. It's November." Bo shakes his head like he's talking to a bunch of kindergarteners. "Dad says there's a cold front coming in right when we leave for camp."

"Great!" I say.

"What? That's not great," Max says.

"Yes it is. Freezing means no scorpions and no moccasins. I'm happy."

"Are the cabins heated?" Max asks.

I hadn't thought of that.

"Do you know which cabin you're in?" Max asks me.

"No, do you?"

"No." Max's eyes widen, and he leans over to whisper. "What if we're in the same cabin with Mason Higgins? Not to be mean, but his clothes will smell up the whole cabin. And we'll be trapped inside."

I hadn't thought of that, either. My brain invents more things to worry about. "What if we get a mean cabin-dad? What if he makes us keep the windows shut and we all die in our sleep because of the air quality?"

"Dudes!" Bo says. "Calm down. You don't have to worry about that."

"How do you know?" Max asks.

"Because I know," Bo says. Then he leans over and whispers. "I know things I'm not supposed to know. Since my dad volunteered to be a cabin-dad, I saw the cabin assignment list that was emailed to him last night. But you can't tell anyone."

We all pause and look around the cafeteria to make sure no one can hear. The girls are talking so loud, we're safe.

Bo whispers so hard he spits. "Mrs. Dixie put you both in our cabin. *My dad*'s our cabin-dad."

I can't contain my pure joy. "Woo-hoo!" I jump up. I'm dancing a little. Shaking my derriere. Max is happy-dancing, too, but he is definitely cheering more loudly than me, which is why Mr. Grodie the gym teacher marches over.

"There is no excuse for this kind of hoopla in the cafeteria. No excuse!"

Actually, there is, I want to say. Instead, I go for a more Pierre-the-Humble approach. "I'm sorry, Mr. Grodie. We're just really happy."

"Well, you just got your entire table a red card." He pulls out a red Uno card and slaps it down on the table. "Red Card!" he shouts. "No talking!"

"Pee-air!" Megan yells. Her screeching voice curdles my earwax even though she's way at the far end of the table.

"That includes you, Megan," Mr. Grodie says, and walks away like a satisfied T-Rex.

I feel bad about getting our whole table a red card. Teachers have a way of making you feel like happiness is a gateway to trouble.

"Pee-air. Pee-air!" Someone whispers.

It's Katelyn, whispering like that possessed girl in Ghostbusters. "Pee-aaaaairr."

"What?" I whisper back.

"Megan wants you to know that you're not a nice person."

I am, too, a nice person, I want to say. *I'm way nicer than you, snootie nose.*

But that wouldn't be nice. So I turn around and shrug at Bo. Even Bo is mad at me. The Red Card sure knows how to ruin an appetite.

ႭꙨႭ

We're in the middle of reading about the Boston Tea Party when Principal Honey makes an announcement on the loudspeaker.

"Will all the fifth grade classes please make their way to the cafeteria for an assembly? All fifth graders, leave your belongings in class and come to the cafeteria for a special assembly."

"What do you think it is?" Max asks me.

"I don't know. But I'm not finished with my chapter yet, and now I'm going to have even more homework."

"Hurry! I want to be at the front of the line!"

I push in my chair and watch the kids shove their way past desks. Papers and pencils are scattered on the floor. Kids are jostling each other, and I can't say why. They don't even know what the heck is in the cafeteria. I must admit, I'm a little excited. But for all we know, there could be a giant roach farm in the cafeteria.

For the record, I'm okay with that. I'm just saying that kids are gullible. And we're marching through the hallway like Gullible's Travels.

"Move back," I hear Bo say. "I'm saving room for Pierre!"

I see Claire's face for a split second before she whips around and her ponytail swats my nose.

"No cut-sies! Cut-sies aren't allowed, Bo."

"You cut all the time."

"I do not!"

I'm about to interrupt and tell them I'm fine where I am when the other fifth grade classes join ours in the hallway. Suddenly, everyone starts pushing forward and kind of bouncing like we're all running on our tippy-toes.

"Holy wildebeest," I mumble. It's like The Great Migration in Africa in here. I look to my right and see a girl with glasses from another class giving me a strange look.

"Did you call me a wildebeest?"

"No." Why would I call her a wildebeest? I don't even know her.

"Did you call *her* a wildebeest?" The girl points to Claire in front of me.

"No! I was talking to myself."

"Yeah. Right." The girl pushes her glasses up on her nose and hurries away.

I'm half-relieved and half-filled with dread that this little misunderstanding is going to haunt me. That's the way fifth grade is. You practically have to creep around corners because you never know who's going to get mad at you.

But my curiosity is making me excited, too. The front of the herd starts squealing and hooting at the end of the hall. When I get to the cafeteria, I see what all the ruckus is about.

About ten teenage girls in short skirts and tall white hats are standing on the stage with their arms locked together at the elbows. They're standing there like soldiers. Very nice-looking soldiers.

"Pierre! Pierre!" I hear Bo calling me. I find him and Max near the front of the cafeteria, waving me over. Somehow, they've saved a space on the floor for me. I sneak over and join them.

"They're girls!" Max says. His face is red and his eyes are practically shooting fireworks. Max is more experienced than me. A lot of girls have had crushes on him since the third grade.

"I think they're the Dancettes from the middle school," Bo says. "My sister is always talking about them. She's going to try out for dance team next year."

"Aren't they cold?" I ask. Their legs are bare, and their uniforms don't have sleeves.

"Nah," Bo says. "My sister says they perform at football games, and they do high kicks and everything to keep warm. And they've got those white boots. Boots are warm."

Principal Honey walks onto the stage and shushes everyone.

"Today, we have two surprises for you. The eighth grade Dancettes from the middle school are here to perform. Girls, you can look forward to trying out for the team in seventh grade. Right, ladies?"

The whole line of dancers nod their heads, like robots. It's strangely pretty.

"And after their performance, they'll talk about middle school extra-curricular activities that will keep you physically fit throughout middle school."

That's when I notice three buff men standing at the edge of the stage.

"Our second surprise is so exciting," Principal Honey says. "We also have special visitors from the *military*. Lance Corporal Bacon will tell you about life as a soldier."

"Bacon?" I whisper to Bo. "Did she say bacon?" The cafeteria always makes me hungry.

"Gross," Bo says, holding his stomach. Bo is very dramatic about his vegetarian status, and tells the cafeteria lady she shouldn't serve "dead-cow" and "dead-piggies."

I watched the hamburger documentary, too, and I secretly cried a tiny bit about the way the animals were treated, but what can I do? My Papa is French, and his cooking makes everything taste like Heaven Café. Even baby cows and rabbits.

Lots of students start laughing at Lance Corporal Bacon's name, which makes Principal Honey clap her hands five times and give us the stern eye. "Lance Corporal Bacon and his new recruits are going to share with us more tips about how to stay physically fit," she says.

Everyone cheers, especially the boys. Except Bo.

"Are you okay?" I ask.

"I'm a pacifist."

"A what?" Max asks.

"I'm for peace, not war!" Bo says.

I guess I'm a pacifist, too, but since I just learned the word, I don't say anything.

"Well," I say, "you can at least enjoy the dancers."

"Shhh!" Mrs. Dixie shushes us and points to the stage. The music starts, and the girls start kicking their boots so high, I hope none of them gets a bloody nose.

It is also a little embarrassing. After all, the girls are wearing short skirts and we're all sitting on the floor looking up at them. Their underthings match. I look around to see if anyone else seems embarrassed. But no. Max is staring at the soldiers and Bo is chewing on a hangnail and looking bored.

How can anyone be bored when ten nice-to-look-at Dancettes are doing high-kicks all for you? After a few minutes, I'm not embarrassed anymore. They are very talented. I think I would snap my legs in two if I tried to dance like that.

At dinner, I tell Mom about the Dancettes.

"I'm not in love, but you know, it's not every day that you get to see dancers do high-kicks."

"I never get to see dancers do high-kicks," Papa says.

"Papa," Mom says, and shakes her head. "Why would they bring dancers *and* soldiers to the elementary school?" Mom asks. "Are they trying to suggest that girls should be dancers and that boys should be soldiers? Because you know, girls can be—"

"I know," I say. "Girls can be anything they want to be."

"Hey, if I were in the audience," Papa laughs, "I'd be more interested in being a dancer than a soldier."

Mom laughs, too. "So I guess the boys really liked the Dancettes, then?"

"No. Not really. They were more interested in the soldiers. They did some pushups and one guy lifted a kid over his head."

I don't tell Mom that the kid tooted on the soldier's head. We are at the table, after all.

"I'm sure the boys were secretly wishing they could be a little more like the girls," Mom says.

I can't help laughing. I laugh so long, I have to hold my aching stomach. "Let me tell you, Mom, from years of experience that most of the boys think that girls are disgusting and terrible and useless."

Once those words come out of my mouth, they don't sound as funny as I thought they'd be.

Mom raises her eyebrows. So I keep talking because I know she's worried about my brain.

"In *Calvin & Hobbes*, Calvin says that girls are very *very* good...for being shipped to Pluto. Wasn't that funny?" She still doesn't smile, so I keep talking. "Of course, *I* don't think girls are disgusting, but there are a few I wouldn't miss if they went to Pluto."

"Disgusting, terrible, and useless?" Mom says. "No no no no."

"I said *most* boys. Not me. I just think girls are...unpredictable. They're nice to you one minute, and the next minute, they're telling the whole class you wiped your boogers on the carpet."

"Oh, *bleh*," Mom says.

"Tell me about it," I say. "And I *told* everyone it wasn't even my booger."

CHAPTER 8

The Big Day

WHY IS IT that whenever there's a big, spectacular day ahead of you, and you absolutely need to go to sleep, you stay up all night telling yourself to go to sleep already? It happens the night before a plane trip to France, before the first day of school, before a whole day at Six Flags. And yesterday, it happened again.

I was supposed to wake up refreshed and with all the time in the world to shower and get dressed in my Not So Lucky Jeans and brand new hiking shoes. *Mais non!* Nope. No sir-ee. Because I had a terrible case of insomnia.

I counted sheep. I counted Stormtroopers. I built an entire Minecraft castle in my head and watched it burn to the ground. No matter what I did, I couldn't get to sleep. I went to the bathroom, read a little *Calvin & Hobbes*, and was about to trudge to bed again when I heard Mom and Papa downstairs.

I crept half-way down the stairs and sat on my favorite step.

"We hear you, Pierre," Mom said. "What's wrong?"

"I can't fall asleep."

"*C'est normal*," Papa said. "It's all the excitement."

"Yeah, it's normal," Mom said. "What's not normal is the weather. Look." She pointed to her laptop screen.

I walked into the kitchen. She was pointing at the weather forecast for the week. It didn't look good. Freezing temperatures. Thunderstorms. High winds.

"It's a little normal," Papa said. "It *is* November."

"In *Texas*," Mom said.

"Do you think they'll cancel the camping trip?" I asked. They wouldn't. They couldn't!

"I emailed your principal, and everything's still on so far. She said they're keeping an eye on the weather." Mom looked worried.

"You'll be fine. Everything will be fine," Papa said, but I think he was talking to Mom more than to me.

"Well, everything's packed in the trunk for the morning. I'll let you sleep in a bit. You don't have to be at school until eight." Mom ruffled my hair and turned me toward the stairs.

I stayed awake in bed for another million hours, imagining all sorts of weather-related horrors that might happen at Adventure Camp. An ice storm in the middle of our hike. A sudden, heavy snowfall that buries our cabin. Katelyn dropping the canoe paddle in the lake.

Of course, I saved everyone by jumping in the lake and pulling the boat to shore with a rope and my bare teeth. The more dangerous the adventure, the more excited and awake I was.

I blinked, and now it's morning. But I'm not late to school. What I am is sleepy. I'm cold and sleepy, and Mom has to wake me up three times.

"The temperature dropped twenty degrees overnight," Papa says in the car. "Cold weather is good for you. It builds character."

"I might build so much character at camp, you won't recognize me."

We pull into the school parking lot, and a ton of other parents are there, unloading sleeping bags and suitcases from their cars. Half the fifth graders look like zombie-popsicles, trudging their way to the school doors.

Papa helps me find my name on the cabin list: the Bluebonnet Cabin. I survey the blacktop for the drop-off locations and lug my duffel bag to the man holding a Bluebonnet poster.

The drop-off spot is right between the Prairie Grass Cabin and the Weed Cabin.

Papa chuckles as the man takes my sleeping bag from him.

"I'm Charlie, Tyler's dad," he says, and shakes Papa's hand. Mr. Charlie has impressive muscles under his camouflage army coat.

"I'm one of the cabin-dads. We're gonna have a great time. Don't you worry."

Papa grins and raises one eyebrow. "You have a Weed cabin?"

Mr. Charlie stares at us.

This is not appropriate humor, I want to tell Papa.

"All the cabins are named after indigenous plants of Texas," Mr. Charlie says.

"Ahh," says Papa. "It was a joke. I'm French," he shrugs. Then he leans over and gives me *bisous*—two kisses on the cheek. "Mom packed you extra everything," he whispers. "Have a good time. And don't lose your flashlight."

I hug him. I don't care if other boys stare.

"*Je t'aime*, Papa."

"I love you, too."

I watch Papa walk back to the car. I notice all the other kids are hugging their parents, too. I'm nervous. I'm excited. I want to skip and sing to the bus. I miss Mom. Sometimes, your feelings are in such a tangle, you can't straighten out your heart from your brain. This is one of those times.

☙❧

"Hello, darling!" the bus lady says when I follow Max and Bo onto the bus. Max smiles and pokes Bo in the back. They're waiting.

We all know what's coming.

"Pretty curls for a pretty girl!" the bus lady sings.

"Thanks," I mumble, and push Max forward. Bo and Max kind of giggle, like they're not sure if I'm going to finally be offended. But actually, I don't mind. Pretty is not a girl-word, right? And besides, we're *Going. To. Camp!*

Max and Bo and I like to sit in the very back seat and jump up every time the bus hits a bump. The airlift is epic. We all get bruises on our butts, but we can't stop laughing.

A dozen kids are assigned to each cabin, and we all have to sit with our cabin groups on the bus so the cabin-dads can keep track of us. Max elbows my arm when Mason Higgins climbs onto our bus.

I must be cursed. Three whole days without having to worry about getting the Stinky Chair, and what do I get? The creator, himself.

"Mason Higgins? Over here," Mr. Robert says. I call Bo's dad "Robert," but on the school trip, it's "Mr. Robert."

Mason plops down on the seat in front of us.

Max leans over me and whispers to Bo, "Why didn't you tell us that Mason's in our cabin?"

"I didn't know until this morning. Then I forgot."

"How could you forget?" Max stops to sniff the air quality. We all take a few whiffs. I can't detect anything. "Well, he's going to get us all in trouble for cussing."

"Don't worry," I whisper. "We have to take a shower every night, remember? And I don't think he'll cuss because Mr. Charlie seems pretty strict. I think he was in the army."

"Great," Bo says.

I don't know what everyone else is thinking, but I'm thinking this is going to be one exciting trip. I look out the window at the crowds of kids getting onto the other two busses. I don't see my crush, Cynthia. *She's new,* I tell myself. *Her parents probably didn't let her come.*

When the bus pulls out of the school parking lot, Bo cheers up and starts singing the most annoying, and therefore the best, camp song in history. "One hundred bottles of pop on the wall, one hundred bottles of pop! Take one down, pass it around, ninety-nine bottles of pop on the wall!" It sounds more like howling than singing, but I don't care. We're finally on our way to Adventure Camp, where Pierre the Bold will face colossal challenges and unexpected perils. And triumph!

CHAPTER 9

Don't Kill Anything

THE CELEBRATION doesn't last long.

Mr. Charlie stops our song when we're only on seventy-eight bottles of pop on the wall. He sounds pretty grumpy. Then Bo's dad, Mr. Robert, tells Mr. Charlie that the kids are all happy and that happy kids don't bother him.

Mr. Charlie is not amused.

Mr. Robert works at an organic grocery, wears leather sandals all year, and taught Bo all about pacifism. Mr. Charlie wears camouflage, talks like a bulldog, and tells all the boys to tuck in their shirts.

I'm pretty happy that they're the Bluebonnet cabin-dads. Mr. Robert is nice and fun, and Mr. Charlie will keep the boys from getting too rowdy. Mr. Robert will probably let us stay up late and play the ukulele, and Mr. Charlie will probably save us from a hungry cougar.

Because we can't sing *or* scream, the only logical thing to do for the next few hours is nap. Which we do.

ᴑᴑᴑ

When I wake up, the whole busload of kids is asleep, and we're pulling into the gravel entrance of Adventure Camp.

It looks cold outside, maybe because the trees are shaking in the wind, and the wind is whistling through the bus windows. A bunch of dead leaves twirl around into a huge vortex beside the bus.

"Look, a leaf tornado," I tell Max, but he's asleep. The leaves spin away and splash apart against a tree trunk.

The gravel driveway is so long, I wonder when we'll ever see the Adventure Center. Mr. Robert stands up and lifts his hands to his mouth. Even his loud voice is friendly and soft.

"Sleepy-time's over, kids. Wake up! I have to tell you some important information before we get off the bus."

I poke Bo, who wakes up with drool on his scarf.

Mr. Robert pats the kids' shoulders until they're all yawning awake. "Don't forget everything your teachers told you about respecting the campgrounds, respecting the cabins, and respecting the wildlife and foliage. You remember, right?"

"Yes, Mr. Robert!" the kids all answer, except for Bo, who says "Mr. Dad."

I'm glad Mr. Robert is with us, but I also think Bo is rubbing it in our faces that his dad is here and our dads aren't.

Every time I turn around, it's "Mr. Dad, come here!"

"Hey, Dad, look at this!" "Daddio, can you help me?"

Why can't he just call his dad "Mr. Robert" like the rest of us? I'm not sure why this bothers me. Maybe I should have begged Papa more to be a cabin-dad.

"So remember," Mr. Robert shouts in the bus, "you can't collect anything from Adventure Camp and take it home with you. No rocks. No pine cones. Leave everything on the nature trails alone unless the guide tells you differently. And DON'T KILL ANYTHING, okay?"

"Not even bed bugs?" Tyler calls out. Tyler looks like a miniature Mr. Charlie.

"Bedbugs!" squeal a few kids. "They've got bedbugs?"

"There are *no bedbugs*!" Mr. Charlie booms.

"Charlie's right. Just...don't kill anything, okay?" Mr. Robert says.

"Okay," we answer.

๑◯๑

When I hop off the bus, the cold slaps me in the face and instantly makes my nose run. The cabin-dads and cabin-moms unload the luggage from the busses, and we huddle in our cabin groups to keep warm and wait for directions.

The Prairie Grass Cabin is apparently a girl cabin because a dozen girls near us are doing jumping jacks and chanting, "Prairie Grass Cabin Girls Rule The World! Prairie Grass Cabin Girls Rule The World!"

"What are they doing?" Bo asks.

"Keeping warm," I say. "Maybe we should do jumping jacks, too."

Max and Bo and I do a few jumping jacks.

That's when I see Claire whispering to Tyler and pointing at me. Of course, the first thing I think is *Oh. My. Snog. Claire has a crush on me.*

Of course, I'm wrong.

Claire and Tyler walk over, I stop jumping up and down. I'm warm and toasty already.

"Hey, Pierre," Tyler says. "Claire wants to know why you called her a wildebeest."

"What?" I look at Claire. Her bottom lip is trembling, but she doesn't look like she's about to cry. She looks like she's about to breathe fire. Dragon fire.

I take a step back. "I don't know what you're talking about."

"You do, too!" she says. "Sylvie told me you called me a wildebeest."

"I didn't. I promise." I race through my brain trying to remember who Sylvie is and why she would accuse me.

Claire stares at me and pokes out her lips, clearly trying to decide if I'm guilty or not. I give her my best Pierre the Innocent look. Because I *am* innocent.

I think it works.

Claire finally turns to Tyler and asks, "What *is* a wildebeest?"

"I think it's that animal in *The Lion King*. You know, Hakuna Matata?"

"Oh, the cute little one?"

"No," says Tyler. "The pig with the two tusks. He has a problem with farts."

Everyone laughs because, let's face it—it *is* funny.

"*What*?" Claire shrieks. "That's so mean!"

"But...But..." I stammer. But my innocence doesn't matter. She is one hundred percent furious, and I am "In the House of the Dog," as Papa says.

"Boy, Claire sure does hate you," Max says as Claire stomps over to the girls.

I can't argue with that.

"Are my Bluebonnets ready?" Mr. Robert calls to us, and we grab our bags.

"Gosh. We really need a new name," Max says. "Don't get me wrong—I like bluebonnets. I just don't want to be *called* a Bluebonnet."

"I couldn't agree more," Mr. Charlie says. Mr. Robert smiles, then leads us to our cabin. "Cabin" is a suspicious title for the building.

It's not even made of logs.

The Bluebonnet Cabin is white with blue shutters. Inside, there are twelve bunks and a gleaming white bathroom with three showers, three sinks, and two toilets.

"This isn't a cabin!" screams Bo. "This is a hotel! Where's the rustic cabin?"

While Bo is standing there looking like someone played a cruel joke on him, the rest of us race to claim our bunks. I get a top bunk right next to the bathroom because I have always wanted to sleep in a top bunk. Near a bathroom.

"Woo-hoo!" several of the boys shout. We all throw our stuff on our beds, and Mason and Tyler and Diego start jumping on the mattresses. They're jumping from one bunk bed to another, and the ground is lava.

Mr. Robert grins.

Mr. Charlie's face is red and a fat vein in his neck pokes out. "No jumping on the beds!"

"They're just having fun," Mr. Robert says. "Come on, boys. Let's go to the Main Center to pick up your folders and workbooks." He claps his hands, then rubs them together. "Time to get your science on!"

CHAPTER 10

Pierre the Nature Hunter

WE HAVE TO put on a million clothes to go outside and hike to the Main Center for our first class meeting. It hasn't even been thirty minutes, and I've already lost a glove.

Outside, all the kids look like ants, walking in single file lines from their cabins to the Main Center. The good news is that the sun's out, and it's actually not that cold when you're walking. The bad news is that we're wearing a million clothes.

Morton Elementary has the entire Adventure Camp to itself this week, so it's like school, and it's not like school. I look up at the sky and let the sun warm my face.

"Watch where you're going," Bo says when I run into him.

I open my eyes and step back. "Sorry."

The line has stopped. Too many ants trying to get in the front door.

"I'm hot," Bo says.

"Me, too," I say.

"Me, too," say about ten other kids. We all start shedding our coats and gloves and hats. Mr. Charlie tells us to put our clothes back on before we lose them. Mr. Robert says, "Aw, we'll find a place to leave their things inside. No need for them to be hot."

Mr. Charlie smiles back, but I can see the vein on his neck bulging. I think this trip is building character for Mr. Charlie, too.

Right as we're about to get inside the glass doors, I look to my right, and who do you think I see?

My crush. Cynthia Meadows.

She's here after all! She's listening to another girl and doesn't see me. I can't hear anything Bo or Max is saying. I want to say hello, but suddenly I have to concentrate on walking so much, it's all my brain can handle.

Just as we get to the front doors of the Main Center, Cynthia holds open the doors and sees me behind her.

She smiles!

I smile!

Today is the best day ever.

"Hurry up!" someone shouts. The next thing I know, I'm shoved into a huge room with a hundred other people. Cynthia is somewhere behind me, and Max is handing me a clipboard with worksheets attached.

"Don't lose the pencil," Max says. "It's the only one we get."

"Good Morning, nature enthusiasts!" a woman wearing a safari outfit shouts.

"Good morning!" everyone screams back.

Fifth graders like to scream. I cover my ears.

"I am your Nature Leader, Mrs. Alba, " the woman announces. Then she introduces us to a ton of other people. After several minutes, I begin to think that we've been tricked, because it sounds a whole lot like those assemblies in the cafeteria that start with a thousand people that need to be thanked. The teachers, the parents, the school board, the janitors.

But finally the introductions end, and we're all still awake. Mrs. Alba gives us a few ground rules, and then announces that we'll start our explorations after lunch.

We all eat our sack lunches picnic-style in the huge hall. Papa put the real French mustard on my pastrami sandwich, which means my tongue is on fire and I'm toasty warm. French mustard is way better than American mustard, but I've learned to keep my mouth shut about these kinds of things at school. Fifth graders love to argue about opinions, even when they are clearly wrong.

We're pretty noisy in the lunch hall. Noisy and crunchy, because practically everyone's mom has packed carrots.

"You all sound like starving rabbits," Mr. Sullivan says, "which reminds me of a story."

Everyone's jaws stop mid-crunch because nobody wants to miss a Sullie-story. He tells us about a pet rabbit he had when he was a kid. The rabbit's name was Dracula because its front teeth grew unusually fast. Mr. Sullivan had to file the rabbit's teeth down every week. One day, Dracula escaped his cage and was lost in the giant garden for two weeks. The only reason Mr. Sullivan found Dracula was because its teeth had grown right into the ground. Mr. Sullivan had to pull that rabbit from the soil, just like a carrot. True story.

After lunch, the Nature Leaders split us into groups.

"The Bluebonnets and the Sagebrush will go canoeing and fishing today, and tomorrow, we'll team up with another cabin and go hiking to collect fauna and flora data," Mrs. Alba says.

We'll hike on trails and record scat and collect owl vomit (which we are already experts at) to dissect in the Main Center.

I'm going to be a scientist, so this schedule makes me so happy, I can't stand it. I'm bouncing on my toes, which makes me look not very serious about science. This is another example of how my body and my brain are sometimes at war.

The fifth grade teachers are all hanging out at the side of the room watching us. It's like a big vacation for them, because now the cabin-dads and cabin-moms have to keep the kids in line, and the Nature Leaders have to teach us.

I'm considering being a scientist *and* a fifth grade teacher so I can take my students to Adventure Camp and have three whole days of fun.

Mrs. Alba is our Nature Leader, which I think is lucky because she has big round glasses and a grandmother smile. "Bluebonnets and Sagebrush," she says, "let's head to the lake!" Mrs. Dixie follows our team to the lake.

At the shore, Mrs. Alba chooses a partner for each of us. I'm hoping that I get Max or Bo, but she takes one look at my curls and pairs me with a girl named Sharee. Sharee was in kindergarten class with me. All I remember about her is that she liked crayons with perfect tips.

"Hi, Pierre!" she says. She's smiling, but she looks nervous.

"Hi, Sharee."

"Have you ever been in a canoe?"

"No. Have you?"

"Nope." She swallows hard and grins again. "I hope we don't drown."

Maybe not *all* the girls in fifth grade are mean.

First, we have to learn about canoe safety. We write down a ton of instructions on our worksheets: Crouch to get on the canoe. Avoid jerky movements. Always wear a lifejacket. Standing in the canoe is forbidden. A paddle is not a weapon.

"Don't forget to put your names on every single worksheet!" Mrs. Dixie says. "Remember, your clipboards will be turned in at the end of camp for a grade."

"My stomach feels dizzy," Sharee says.

"Don't worry," I say. I sign my Canoe Safety worksheet and show Sharee. Pierre the Lifejacket.

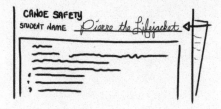

Sharee smiles.

I sign the second worksheet and show Sharee. Pierre the Fantastic Flying Fish.

Sharee laughs. "You're weird."

"Merci," I say, and take a deep bow. "That means thank you."

I look over at Max, who has Megan as his partner.

"You're doing it wrong!" Megan says. "We have to carry the canoe upside down! Let me show you how."

Max gives me a scared look. Poor Max.

For the next two hours, Sharee and I paddle around the lake. It starts out rough. At first, I can't make the canoe stop spinning in circles. Then Sharee almost loses her grip on the paddle, and when she leans over, the canoe wobbles so much, I'm confident we're going to drown.

But before long, we get the hang of it. We paddle across the whole lake, stopping a few times to record all the insects and animals we see.

"Hey, Pierre!" Max shouts. He paddles his canoe closer to us. He's red-faced and sweaty, but looks happy enough. Megan is still wearing her coat under her lifejacket. Her sleeves are so puffy that her arms stick out to the sides.

"Don't crash!" Megan says, clutching her clipboard on her lap.

"There's a seaweed swamp over near that big tree," Max calls to me. "Want to go paddle to it?"

"Sure!" Sharee says before I can even answer. She's a pretty good canoe partner.

"No! What if we get stuck in it?" Megan says. "I can't paddle right with these dumb sleeves."

"We'll be fine," Max says.

I give them a thumbs up. "We need more flora on our list. Right, Sharee?"

"Come on!" she says, and paddles so fast, the water splashes onto my face.

Megan doesn't argue. We paddle right into the green, swampy seaweed, which probably isn't really seaweed since we're in a lake.

"Look!" Max says, lifting his paddle. He's caught a giant spoonful of slimy spinach.

"Oooh, gross!" We all laugh, even Megan. Sharee sketches a picture of the green gunk so we can copy it on our worksheets later. Max and I come up with a brilliant plan to get stuck in the gunk so we can escape like heroes, but no matter how hard we try, our canoes slice easily through the muck.

On our way back to the shore, we see Mrs. Dixie sitting all alone in a canoe. She's not frowning. She's not looking at the kids. She's not even telling Bo and Hunter to stop paddle-fighting. She's closing her eyes and smiling. I think she looks nice there in the sun. Someone should paint her picture and give it to her when she's having a bad day.

Our next activity is fishing. By the time we put away our canoes and walk out to the fishing pier, the clouds have blown in and the air is cold again. Canoeing with Sharee was fun, but I'm glad to be back with Bo and Max again.

"Why do we have to fish?" Bo asks Mrs. Alba. "I'm a vegetarian, you know."

Mrs. Alba hands a fishing pole to all the Bluebonnets as we march onto the pier. "So am I!" she smiles. "Don't worry. We're not going to eat the fish. We catch and release. It doesn't really hurt them."

"Yeahhh," Bo says, as he examines a metal fishing hook. "Right. This looks pretty painful." He sits down on the pier instead of grabbing a fishing pole.

We spear little chunks of hotdog on our hooks and throw our lines into the water. Right away, the fish nibble our hotdog bait right off the hooks. We keep baiting our hooks, but they're too clever. It's like a fish buffet.

"I'm going to catch twenty fish," I say.

"I'm going to catch thirty," Max says.

"Go away, fishies!" Bo shouts and sloshes the water with his fingers. "Run for your lives!"

After half an hour, no one has caught a fish except for Mr. Charlie, who looks pretty satisfied with himself.

"Why don't you give it a try?" Mrs. Alba asks Bo.

"I don't think so..."

"Go ahead, son," Mr. Robert says. "We eat fish at home. It's not any different."

I hand Bo my useless rod. "Here. Take my fishing pole."

"Okay."

Thirty seconds later, Bo reels in a fish as big as my foot. Just my luck.

"I caught one! I caught one!" Bo shouts. Everyone cheers, even me, because I'm a good friend, even when I'm jealous. Mr. Robert helps Bo unhook the fish.

Mr. Sullivan claps his hands and says, "Well done, Bo! Don't throw it back until you kiss it."

"What?" Bo grins, because kissing a fish is just the sort of thing Bo would dare someone else to do.

"Fish love to be kissed," Mr. Sullivan says. "Don't they?"

I think Mr. Sullivan wants the Nature Leader to agree, but Mrs. Alba just stands there frozen-faced and wide-eyed. The fish is squirming and its tail is flip-flapping, so Mr. Robert helps Bo keep it from leaping onto the pier.

"Kiss it, right on its fishy lips," Mr. Sullivan sings.

"Disgusting! Gross!" the kids are yelling.

"Do it!" I say. I don't know what's wrong with me. I simply *have* to see him kiss the fish. "Do it! Do it!"

Bo leans over and plants a big kiss right on the fish's mouth. He grins at his dad, and everyone cheers.

"Be free, fish!" he shouts, and throws the fish into the lake.

Another fantastic flying fish.

CHAPTER 11

Ghost Stories

ONE THING YOU have to know about French people is that they take food seriously. You can't have the TV on when you're eating. EVER. You always eat with a fork *and* knife, and you put your slice of bread on the table, never on the plate. There are other rules, like never taking a bite until Mom takes her first bite, even if I'm starving. But that's okay, because another thing you should know is that Papa is the best cook in Texas, guaranteed.

Maybe even the United States.

That's why I was nervous about the meals at camp. I'm used to *quality* food. But all my fears evaporate as soon as we walk into the dining hall. I could lick the air, it smells so good.

I take the lasagna and broccoli and sit with Bo and Max at the Bluebonnet table.

"Is that a meat lasagna?" Bo says. His lips are curled in disgust.

"I don't know and I don't care," I say, shoveling a huge spoonful in my mouth because Mom is nowhere in sight. My cheeks tingle with cheesy goodness.

"I've got a special vegetarian meal," Bo says. His plate is full of pasta and teriyaki tofu. "This is the best camp ever."

Max and I nod.

Before we can swallow our first bite, Mason Higgins sits down at our table with his own plate of lasagna. I'm hoping the cheesy aroma will conquer any Mason aroma. Just to be sure, I hunker down over my plate so my nose almost touches the cheese.

Bo and Max take my lead. We look kind of silly carrying on a conversation with our noses in our food, but this is an emergency. Self-preservation. And we don't want to be mean to Mason Higgins. He might retaliate and call us dirty names. Or worse. He might crawl inside our sleeping bags.

My nose itches just thinking about it.

"You boys must be starving!" Mr. Robert says. Mr. Charlie and Mr. Robert sit down on either side of Mason.

After a few seconds, Mr. Robert understands our stinky crisis. He freezes and sniffs the air.

Mr. Charlie takes a few whiffs, too, and stops when he turns toward Mason. Finally, the adults are learning a thing or two about the cruelties of fifth grade.

"Well," Mr. Charlie says, and clears his throat. "I sure am looking forward to a hot shower tonight. How about you boys?"

I agree. Enthusiastically.

☯

By the time, we've all had our showers and brushed our teeth and turned the heater as high as it goes, my stomach starts to crunch.

"It's the lasagna," Bo says. "Maybe the meat was bad."

"It's the excitement," Max says. "It's called the jitters."

"It's the weather," Mr. Robert says. "Don't worry. We're safe and warm inside."

But I know what it is. It's the whole, long night ahead of me. I'm wearing my favorite Star Wars pajamas and my Minecraft slippers, but they're no help. I'm starting to regret my decision not to pack the emergency Biggies that Mom bought.

I'm also regretting my decision to sleep in the top bunk. It was the opportunity of a lifetime. But if there's an accident, how can I sneak down now without anyone noticing?

I wish I could have a conversation with my bladder and give it a serious lecture about being dependable for once.

But I don't speak bladder. I can hardly speak French.

Mr. Charlie tells me I just need sleep and announces to everyone that we're having Lights Out at nine. But Mr. Sullivan stops by and tells us a real-life ghost story. First, we have to get into our sleeping bags. Then, he turns off the cabin light and shines his flashlight right under his chin. It's the creepiest thing I've ever seen.

If you've never seen your teacher like this, don't. It is not worth the long-term trauma.

"A few years ago," he begins, "while I was staying at my Uncle Doug's house, I was feeling peckish and went down to make a midnight snack. I found a hamburger in the fridge that looked pretty good, so I put it in the microwave."

Mr. Sullivan slows his voice to a creepy crawl. "And while I was waiting, I heard a whine. A slow, painful whine that sounded like this, 'noooooooooooo'."

"It was the microwave," someone says.

"I *wish* it was the microwave. I took the hamburger out of the microwave and sat down to eat it. But I kept hearing that same sound, 'Noooooooooo. Nooooo.' I leaned over my plate. The whine was coming from my hamburger!"

The kids laugh nervously.

"You think it's funny? You won't! I slowly lifted the bun off the top, and the hamburger meat was steaming. *Whistling*. It seemed to be begging me, 'nooooooo.' It didn't want me to eat it."

"Did you eat it?" I ask.

"What do you think?"

"You ate it?!"

"The end!" Mason says. I laugh again, but my heart is hugging my throat.

"*Not* the end!" Mr. Sullivan says. "I climbed upstairs and went to bed. But I couldn't sleep well because I kept hearing 'nooooo', 'nooooo', 'nooooo.' *It's just the steam from the hamburger*, I told myself. That night, I dreamed of a giant hamburger blob. He raised his big, meaty, blobby arms above me and said, "I'm the ghost of hamburgers past! I warned you! Now, I'll never go away."

Mr. Sullivan's flashlight flickers under his chin.

"He chased me until I woke up. And my legs were still moving. Trying to get away. The next morning, I walked downstairs, and do you know what I saw?"

"What?" everyone says. We're whispering. We're scared.

"The *same* hamburger. On a plate, in the middle of the table. Still steaming. Still whistling the faintest cry, 'nooooo!'"

We're all silent, letting the creepiness shiver through our bones.

"I thought you ate the hamburger," Max says.

"I did. Time for bed!" he says cheerfully. And just like that, Mr. Sullivan turns off his flashlight and leaves the Bluebonnet Cabin.

Visions of the blobby hamburger ghost dance in the darkness. I'm sure I'm not the only one who's shivering.

"See?" Bo finally says. "There *are* benefits to being a vegetarian."

Of course, Mr. Robert turns the lights back on because a couple of the boys are seriously freaked out.

"I was going to save these gifts until tomorrow night," Mr. Robert says, "but here. These will make you feel safe." He brings out little bags of itty-bitty flashlights with elastic bands that fit perfectly over the tips of our fingers. We each get ten colorful finger-lights.

He turns off the big cabin light, and suddenly the whole room is filled with a rainbow of tiny lights.

For the rest of the night, we make light shows on the ceiling.

Max goes to sleep first. Then Bo.

And—*PZZT! Toot! Phlubt!*—the cabin is full of sounds.

I stare at my finger-lights dancing on the ceiling, mouthing *Don't fall asleep. Don't fall asleep. Don't fall asleep.* I climb down the ladder and go to the restroom three times. Practice runs, in case I have to make an emergency trip in the middle of the night. After what seems like an eternity, the owls have stopped hooting and one of my finger lights burns out. My eyelids can't take the strain anymore, so I turn off the rest of my finger-lights and tell my body, "*Bonne nuit.* Don't let me down."

CHAPTER 12

Accidents Happen

"WAKE UP!" a voice shouts. "Wake up! Wake up!"

Oh no! I think. Inside my dark sleeping bag, I open one eye. *What have I done?* I reach beneath me and feel the sleeping bag.

Dry. Dry.

My pajama bottoms? Dry.

No accident! *Hurray!* I want to holler. Success! I could throw myself a parade, I'm so happy. A ginormous parade, with elephants and cheers and ticker tape streaming down the whole street. Today should be declared Pierre François High and Dry Day! Hooray!

Actually, it's not my conscience shouting. It's some other kid screaming in the cabin.

I poke my head out of my sleeping bag in the too-bright light.

"Wake up!" Tyler says, jumping from bunk to bunk.

I duck just in time. My mattress bounces me up like a trampoline.

"Wake up, soldier!" Diego says. He's following Tyler and lands on my bed for an instant. I try to grab his ankle, but he's too fast.

He's already on Max's bed.

I rub my eyes and watch Tyler and Diego hooting and laughing as they bounce around the room. The only person safe is Mason Higgins. No one jumps on his bed. Even though we all had showers, something sour still hangs onto Mason's clothes and towels, and we're all a little nervous that we'll catch it.

"What. Are. You. DOING?" Bo hollers at Tyler and Diego. Bo is not a morning person.

"My dad and Mr. Robert went to the Main Center for coffee," Tyler says. "We all have to be up and dressed by the time they get back."

I sit up and scratch my head. Immediately, my arms are popsicles with goose bumps.

Diego bounces across my bed again. "Hey, look at Pierre's hair!"

I reach up and feel the static electricity in my hair. I'm having an Einstein-hair morning.

Everyone looks at me and laughs. I don't mind. I'm in a great mood.

"Yeah yeah yeah," I say, grinning. "You won't be laughing when I win the Nobel Prize."

They shrug and stop laughing because nobody knows what I'm talking about. That's my favorite tactic: confuse and distractify.

"Why. Is. It. So. COLD?" Bo hollers again.

"It's thirty-eight degrees outside," Tyler says.

"How do you know?" I ask.

"Mr. Robert said. You have to warm up like us. See? We're not cold anymore." Tyler pauses on an empty bunk to pose like a weight-lifter.

Bo rubs his eyes. Evidently, it sounds like a good idea to him because he climbs to a top bunk and says, "I'm it!"

"Or you could take a hot shower," I suggest. But I'm too late. They're already chasing each other. I barely make it off my mattress before they land on me.

The floor is so cold, it curls my toes.

I need privacy to get dressed. Maybe it's because I'm not involved in team sports, but I'm not used to seeing other boys in their underwear. So I race to the bathroom and get dressed in world-record speed. Then I dance in the middle of the cabin and keep score. Tyler, Diego, and Bo are super-ninjas, running across treetops, fleeing the Frost Dragon.

I don't even tell them that they're going to get in trouble for not getting dressed because this is what camp is all about. We're making memories here.

ㅇ═ㅇ

After breakfast, we're back to work again.

"Are you ready for a long hike?" Mrs. Alba asks.

"No!" we all say.

Even though I'm dressed like an Eskimo, my cheeks are still aching from the short walk to the Main Center. The Bluebonnets and the Sagebrush get a new pack of worksheets for our clipboards.

"It's so thick!" Max says.

I flip through the packet. There are lots and lots of empty lines and boxes to fill. Max's jaw drops and he looks at me for sympathy. But I don't mind. It's like the world's biggest treasure hunt.

I write my name on the first page. Pierre the Cheese.

"Why'd you write that?" Max asks me.

"Because he's weird," Bo says.

"Thank you," I say, and take a bow. Then I do the other pages. Pierre the Cardboard. Pierre the Particle Board. Pierre the Sad Sad Sad Sodapop. Pierre the Epic Yolo Face that Rolled Off a Cliff.

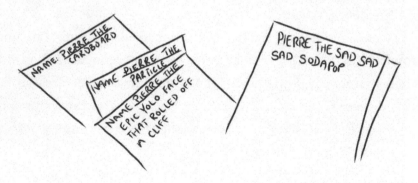

While our cabin-dads are getting another cup of coffee, Mrs. Alba gives us directions and reminds us to respect nature and the trails. She's like Mother Nature's mother. Grandmother Nature.

"We're going to conduct experiments on soil, collect some animal scat, and hopefully observe a few animals. You'd be surprised at how many birds and small creatures you'll see, even in cold weather."

Then Mrs. Alba leaves the room to get something, which of course sets off a tsunami of chatting. Not being able to talk at school is like having to hold your breath under water. At some point, you have to come up for air.

"Stop yelling!" Mr. Sullivan's voice booms.

I didn't even know he was in the room with us.

We all turn around and see him standing there. He never sticks around for long at camp, I guess because there are so many kids he has to startle. But maybe he'll stay and tell us a story on our hike.

Here is one thing you have to know about Mr. Sullivan: when he is serious, he is really really serious. You don't joke around with Mr. Sullivan when his eyebrows are raised. Like they are now.

I cover my funny names with my forearm because now is not the time for humor.

"Before you go outside on the trails," he says, "I want to be sure that you're clear about how to act. You might get separated from your Nature Leader on the trail, but keep walking, stay on the trail, and you'll end up with everyone else at the end."

He makes it sounds like we're climbing Mount Everest.

"Rocks and sticks are not weapons. Don't play around with those things. You'll be getting plastic vials, thermometers, and butter knives for cutting samples. Butter knives are not weapons."

It takes all my mental strength to keep my mouth shut. Because butter knives kind of *are* weapons. But I do because I do not feel like risking my life today. Mr. Sullivan holds up a plastic butter knife.

"These utensils are *not toys*. Don't even think about pretending to stab someone. Some people can be jerks with the butter knives. I've known some fifth graders who can act like real jerks."

Mr. Sullivan is super serious. I've never heard him say "jerk" before, and I wonder if that's even allowed. I look around for the cabin-dads, but Yoda-Sullivan is very wise: *all alone, we are.*

"Do *not* be a jerk," he says. Everyone nods. He nods back at us. Considering he's been a teacher for forty years, I guess he has seen a lot of jerky kids.

Then he smiles really big and pats Sharee on the shoulder. "Great! Have a fun time on the trails!"

ᴑᴑᴑ

On the Wild West Trail, Max and Bo and Sharee and I team up to fill out our worksheets on Flora and Fauna of North Texas. Sharee is hogging the butter knife. I kind of wish Cynthia was with our team instead. Cynthia wouldn't hog the butter knife. I haven't seen her since we first got here, and I wonder if she's cold. I wonder if she's canoeing in circles on the lake. I wonder if she remembers me.

After thirty minutes, my fingers on my right hand are white and tingly. My missing glove is probably all warm and cozy in the cabin.

"Here's another scat!" Bo calls. "We've got the tracks here, too."

I draw the best picture of poop I can manage. It doesn't look much different from the other poops. Fox scat, deer scat, rabbit scat, they're just wobbly circles on my form.

Max, on the other hand, *Max* can draw realistic poop.

FOX SCAT   DEER SCAT   RABBIT SCAT

Max is the best artist in our class. He pays attention to detail. I hurry up with my sketch so I can watch him draw a hawk. My hawk looks more like a circle with a cross under it. His hawk is like the Mona Lisa with wings.

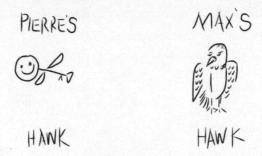

For some reason, we are nearly the last group of kids on the trail. I normally don't mind because I'm used to being the last. I'm a fan of not hurrying. I'm also a fan of double-checking. But halfway through our worksheet packet, I'm a fan of Let's Get The Heck Inside.

"This is a democracy, right?" I say. "I vote let's run the rest of the trail."

"Great idea," Bo says.

We take off running, but we have to stop once to collect a vial of icy water at the Wild West Creek. That's when Mason and Tyler and Hunter catch up with us on the trail. For a minute, we all stand there, staring at each other like we're about to have a stand-off right there on the Wild West Trail.

You know that lonesome flute that plays in every sheriff scene with the bad guy? It's playing in my head. My fingers wiggle by my side. Pierre the Sharpshooter. But instead of a shoot-out, we're going to race to the Main Center. It's our team against theirs.

"Hurry up!" Sharee tells me as I'm screwing on the vial's lid. "They'll beat us. Let's go!"

Then we're running. Racing against those outlaws. I am not a fan of being last, so I'm ahead of everyone. I hear Bo and Max laughing and shouting, which is great because they're not fighting. They haven't fought at all at Adventure Camp. My eyes are streaming tears because of the frigid wind, but I don't look back.

The end of the trail opens up on a wide prairie. I finally stop, drop my clipboard, and put my hands on my knees to catch my breath. To my surprise, Sharee is right behind me.

"Where's...where's...Bo and Max?" I finally get the words out.

"They were behind me."

Suddenly, we hear a watery sound. *SPLOOSH!* And then someone yelling, "AHHHHRGH!"

Someone who sounds like Bo.

Sharee and I look at each other. Then we run a little ways back and see Bo sloshing through the trees.

"I went off the trail and landed in a puddle!" He shouts, shaking his wet jeans.

Max catches up and laughs. "Sorry, Bo."

"It's not funny!" he screams at Max.

I don't laugh because if there's one thing I know, it's that wet pants are not funny.

"Where are the other guys?" I ask.

"I don't think they knew we were racing," Max says, looking down the trail.

By the time we reach the Main Center, Mr. Robert and Mr. Charlie are standing at the door waving everyone inside.

"What happened to you?" Mr. Robert asks Bo.

"I fell in a puddle."

Mr. Robert doesn't even look surprised. "The kids are starting on their experiments with the creek water. Why don't you run to our cabin and get some dry jeans on first?"

Bo shrugs. "I don't have an extra pair. I just have jeans for tomorrow."

"What? I told you to pack extras." Mr. Robert looks up at the sky and sighs.

I have an intense debate in my head that lasts for centuries, but in real life it lasts about two seconds. The consequences are nerve-wracking. I kind of need my pants. But I blurt out, "It's okay, Mr. Robert. I have an extra pair of sweatpants he can borrow. I packed them to sleep in, in case it's too cold."

"Really? You don't mind?" Bo asks.

"That's what friends are for."

Mr. Robert looks at me like I'm Pierre the Saint of Boys in Wet Pants.

"You're sure, Pierre?"

I swallow a not-sure lump in my throat and nod.

"You're a good friend. Hurry up, now. Try to be back in ten minutes."

Bo and I take off for the Bluebonnet Cabin, and I am feeling a little nervous and a little proud. Because how many times do you get to leave school in the middle of the day to rescue your best friend from public humiliation?

CHAPTER 13

A New Kind of Fight

"WE BETTER HURRY," Bo says. "I don't want to miss lunch."

"Lunch?" I say, and open the cabin door. "We still have a whole hour, which is *science* by the way."

"Oh, yeah."

"I want to see those tiny lake thingies swimming under the microscope. I hope Sharee doesn't kill them before we get back."

"It's freezing outside. If they can survive this ice age, they'll live until we get back."

Bo has to jump up and down to get his wet jeans off. He is not a privacy person like I am.

"I'll get the sweatpants," I say, and climb up on my bunk.

Right as I kneel on my bunk and pull my duffel bag closer, my brain has a heart attack. A spider is sitting right on the zipper. I am not normally a scaredy-cat, but this spider is huge. And black. And I think I startled him.

I jump back and fall on my butt. *You're safe,* I tell myself. *You're alive.* But the only thing scarier than seeing a big black spider is *losing sight* of a big black spider you just saw. So I take a breath, get back on my knees, and lean toward the duffel bag again. This guy is humongous and hairy and not happy to see me.

Then he jumps–no, *leaps*–up at me. I am not kidding!

Considering the potentially fatal situation, I think no one could blame me for screaming.

"What happened?" Bo says, running over in just his tidy-whities.

I move backwards in slow motion because even though he's still on my duffel bag, I don't know how far this guy jumps. But as soon as my feet hit the top rung, I leap off the ladder and take cover.

"What's *wrong* with you?" Bo says.

"We have a slight problem. There's a mutant spider on my bag. And the sweatpants are in the bag."

"Oh."

We stand there for a minute. I almost sit down on another kid's bunk, but change my mind because what if there's a whole spider family reunion going on here?

Bo shivers and grabs his elbows. Then he walks over to my ladder. "Are you sure it was a spider? Maybe it was a dust bunny."

"It was *not* a dust bunny," I say. "What are we going to do? We can't hang out here forever."

"Why don't you just brush it off your bag?"

"What? No way!" A jolt of I'd Rather Die shivers through my bones. I am Pierre the Scared. Pierre the Great Big Wimperoo. And I will shout it from the rooftops before I go up that ladder again.

"It's just a spider."

"What if it crawls back up to my bunk? What if it hides in my sleeping bag? Or yours?"

There is only one solution. Bo and I stare at each other.

"Bo, I am deathly afraid of spiders."

"They're not my best friends, either," he says.

"But you're...you're Bo the Brave. Please, *please* would you smash it? I mean, we have to get those sweatpants somehow."

"Well..." He thinks for a few seconds.

"Bo the Brave," I whisper.

"I *am* a pacifist, you know. But, okay, I'll kill it. For you." He steps onto the ladder. "And for the pants. It's cold."

At the top, he turns back to me. "I see it. It's on the handle. It's not *that* big. Give me your shoe."

"I don't want spider guts on my shoe!"

"Well, give me something to smash it. Hurry, before it crawls into your bag."

I spin around and see Mason's orange shoe on the floor.

"Sorry, Mason," I mutter, and hand the shoe to Bo. "Here."

Bo kills the beast on the first blow. He tosses the shoe on the floor and digs in my bag for the sweatpants.

"Thanks, Bo," I say.

"That's okay. Thanks for the sweats."

On the way back to the Main Center, I can't stop thinking about the spider. Bo is quiet, too. "You realize what we've done?" I ask.

"Yeah."

I whisper, "We *killed* nature. We broke the number one rule at Adventure Camp. I'm not a rule-breaker!"

"Don't freak out," Bo says. "It was an emergency. I feel bad about it, too. It *was* kind of a cute spider."

"I wouldn't go that far."

"I'm just trying to respect his memory," Bo says.

"Do you feel guilty?" I ask. "You *are* vegetarian."

"I guess not. It's not like we're out to kill all the spiders in the wilderness. Just the one in our cabin."

"Right."

At the doors to the Main Center, Bo stops me. "Maybe we shouldn't tell anyone."

"Yeah. Let's keep this highly confidential."

"Besides, I'm pretty sure there are hundreds of spider eggs all over this place. You know, the circle of life."

Bo walks inside while I'm thinking this over. Hundreds of spider eggs. Maybe millions.

ᴑ◯ᴑ

To keep the spider-pocalypse off my brain, I am keeping score of all the great memories here that I will tell my children and my grandchildren and my great-grandchildren. I write down all the great memories I can remember:

1. We paddled a canoe to the center of a lake and didn't drown!

2. We collected nature specimens during a cold front and didn't freeze!

3. We escaped a spider ambush and didn't die!

4. I watched my first larvae swimming under a microscope, and named him Timmy!

5. We made s'mores on a bar-b-que pit because it was too cold for a campfire!

6. I defeated my greatest fear and made it through camp without a single accident!

I'm planning ahead with number six because Adventure Camp is almost over. Why not have a positive attitude? I'm a glass-half-full kind of guy.

Which is why I go to the bathroom three times before I go to bed.

ᴑ◯ᴑ

After dinner, all the kids are packing their bags.

"Boys, don't leave anything out except tomorrow's clothes and your toothbrush," Mr. Robert says. "Pack it all up. We're leaving right after breakfast."

But the thunderstorm is making all the kids hyperactive. Tyler and Hunter and Mason are socking each other with pillows.

"Did I get everyone's clipboard and worksheets?" Mr. Charlie says. "Hey! Cut it out!"

Mr. Charlie turns around right as Mason's pillow flings up. In the world's most terrible timing, the pillow socks Mr. Charlie right across the jaw.

Mason's mouth opens in shock. "Holy cra—"

"Crabapple!" I yell over Mason's voice. I can't help it. It's like I *have* to save him or something. What is wrong with me? "Holy crabapple?" I say again.

Everyone freezes. Mr. Charlie's neck vein pokes out so much, I'm afraid it might geyser on us.

"That's it!" he bellows. Just when I think he's going to make us all drop and do a hundred pushups, Mr. Charlie grabs his super-size pillow and says, "Pillow fight!"

"Pillow fight!" we all holler.

We don't even hear the thunder smashing outside the cabin. I swing my pillow a few times, but I spend most of the time hopping from bunk to bunk in the most epic game of tag ever. I am Pierre the Swift Pillow, and I cannot be defeated.

CHAPTER 14

Some Things You Can't Control

I DO NOT REMEMBER falling asleep. But I will never forget waking up. In my sleeping bag cocoon. Dark and damp.

I'm not wet.

I'm drenched. *No, no, no, no, no.*

Blasted urine! Blasted bladder! I bolt up out of my bag like a cartoon Dracula and shout, "EXPLETIVE!"

It's not even night anymore. The cabin lights are on. People are getting dressed. I look down and half the kids in the cabin staring at me.

"Um, what?" Tyler says.

I look down at my pajamas. They're wet. My sleeping bag is wet. My back is wet and my hair is stuck to my scalp.

I'm hot. The vent beside my bed is wheezing out hot air. I sniff my damp sleeves.

Hey! It's not pee, after all.

I'm just sweating! I'm a sweaty pig, and I love it!

"I was just speaking French," I grin at Tyler. "I sometimes do that in my sleep."

Diego jumps from out of nowhere onto my open sleeping bag. "Wake up, ya lazy...eewww!" He lifts one foot and shakes it in the air. "It's wet!"

"Get off my bed!" I swat Diego's other leg. He tiptoes across my bunk and hurries down the ladder.

"You wet your bed?" Hunter says. He throws his head back and laughs. It is a cruel laugh. He could stab me with that laugh.

"No!"

"Gross!" Hunter holds his stomach and laughs some more. "PeePee-air wet his bed!"

That makes the other kids laugh. They try to hide it behind their hands, but I can see them.

"I didn't have an accident! I'm just sweaty!" I point to the vent, but Hunter nods and slings his arm around Tyler.

"All right, PeePee-air. We believe you, PeePee-air."

I need back-up, pronto, before PeePee-air becomes my new nickname. I look around for the cabin-dads, but they're gone. Probably getting coffee again. Even Max and Bo are missing. Probably taking a shower. Where are your friends when you need them?

"Wait till I tell the girls," Hunter says to Tyler.

The lump in my throat turns into a rock, and my eyes start to burn.

"Shut up, Hunter," Mason says.

Everyone looks at Mason, who's stopped packing his stinky pants. Mason looks at me, then stands up. He is so tall, Hunter looks like a gnome in comparison.

"How would you like it if someone teased *you* about having an accident?"

"I *didn't have* an accident!" I say.

"Maybe not." Mason shrugs, like he's not sure he believes me. "But who cares!" he tells Hunter. "It's not his fault! You don't have to *bully* him."

Everyone's still in shock that Mason Higgins is defending me. I'm in shock.

"I'm not a bully," Hunter says.

"It was kind of mean," Diego says, and shrugs at his friends.

"Oh. Well, sorry," Hunter says. "Sorry, Pierre."

"Yeah, sorry Pierre," Tyler says. "No hard feelings."

Mason zips up his bag, puts on his coat, and walks out of the cabin. I'm pretty sure Mason didn't take a shower.

"It really *is* sweat," I say louder. "This vent has dragon breath."

I scramble off the bunk bed, and just like that, the crisis is over. Nobody calls me PeePee-air again.

All because of Mason. Who'd have thought?

When I grab my soap and towel and head to the showers, I'm relieved. But I'm not exactly happy. I know why, and I need to fix it.

ᴑ◯ᴑ

I find Mason sitting on a small bench outside the Main Center.

The fifth graders were supposed to wait inside for the busses back to Morton Elementary, but pancakes and syrup made everyone so hyper, the teachers sent most of us outside to burn off energy.

"Hey Mason," I say.

"Oh, hey," Mason says and scoots his butt over. "Want to sit?"

Sit? I settle for a compromise by putting my foot on the bench and leaning on my knee.

"Hey, I wanted to tell you...thanks for sticking up for me in the cabin." I lift of my hand for a high five. Who cares if he's a little smelly? Maybe he can't help it. He slaps my hand and grins.

"That was nice to stick up for me."

"No problem," Mason says.

I want to do something nice for Mason, too. Maybe I can help him with the stinky pants problem, but what am I supposed to say? I don't even think he knows he smells.

"It really was just sweat. Not, you know...pee." I laugh nervously.

"It's called enuresis. My little brother has the same problem. We have to share a bed. I *hate* when he has an accident. But he hates it even more, 'cause...you know. It's not his fault."

I nod. Maybe that's why his clothes smell. I didn't know he had a brother. Maybe there are a lot of things I don't know.

"It's kind of like you," Mason adds. "You can't help it that you look like a girl."

"Well," I stammer, because it sounds fine when I say it, but it doesn't sound so nice when I hear someone else say it.

But it's true. One time when I was in third grade, I cut my hair really short. Even when I wore my ugly dragon shirt, ladies *still* told me I was going into the wrong restroom. "No, no! Come over here," they'd wave at me, "*this* is the girls' restroom!"

"My Papa's French," I say to Mason. "He says I have French features and that I should be proud of them. I am, but these perfect curls can be annoying sometimes."

"I don't have a dad anymore," Mason says. "But it's okay. He was a jerk."

I have the feeling that Mason is telling me secrets—his little brother's accidents, his mean dad— so I'm not going to tell anyone. Not even Bo and Max. I decide to tell him one, too, even if I'm risking my life.

"Hey, Mason...I should tell you something. Yesterday, there was a spider on my duffel bag, and I had to use your orange shoe to kill it. I'm sorry. It was an emergency."

I hold my breath and wait for him to cuss at me. I've heard him cuss at other kids before, and it is not pleasant.

But Mason just frowns and says, "Oh."

"There's probably spider guts on your shoe now. Aren't you mad?"

"I guess not. I stepped in some poo yesterday, so they were already dirty."

"Oh," I say, looking at my hands. I give them a quick sniff for poo.

Mason pokes my arm. "You like tag, right?"

"Yeah. But nobody plays it anymore."

"Let's play tag tomorrow. I'm tired of Keepie Ball. I always win."

"Okay," I say. "Keepie Ball stinks. Taggers rule."

"Yeah," he says. And suddenly I feel a million times better.

I'm about to go find Max and Bo when I hear my name.

"Pierre!" she says again.

I look to my right, and guess who is *Calling. My. Name*?!

It's Cynthia, and I am not kidding, she has a halo of light around her head. I've never heard her loud voice before, but let me tell you: it is even nicer than her quiet voice.

"Want to play tetherball with me?" she asks.

I think I am dead. Or dreaming. Because how else is this possible?

"Sure!" I say.

I have no idea how to play tetherball. We spend the next few minutes bopping the ball back and forth. She covers a smile when the ball hits my head. I let the ball bang my head a few more times because her smile is nice.

What is *wrong* with me?

Then the busses roll into the parking lot and the teachers start yelling at us to line up.

"Thanks for playing," Cynthia says.

I take a deep bow. "It was a privilege to be beaten by you." That's something my Papa says to Mom on game nights.

Cynthia laughs and runs toward the busses.

I think I'll ask Mom for a tetherball this Christmas because clearly tetherball is the greatest sport ever.

∽◯∾

On the bus ride back to school, Max asks me, "Why do you think Mason smells like pee?"

"Maybe his mom leaves his wet clothes in the laundry," Bo says. "My mom did that once, and it smelled so bad, I thought my nose would fall off."

I think about Mason's little brother, and that peed-on bed, and how nice it would be to have a big brother to remind you that some things are not your fault, even if the evidence says otherwise. I think about all the mean things we've said about Mason for the past few months.

From now on, I'm going to be better. I don't know if that's what French people do, but it's what Pierre the Grateful does.

Max shakes his head. "Can't he smell himself?"

❖ 114 ❖

"Give him a break," I say. "Maybe it's puberty. Maybe we'll *all* smell bad when we get our growth spurt."

"Oh no. I don't want to get all hairy," Bo says.

"Dad says your arms grow long like orangutans and you sweat behind your knees," Max says. "Gross."

"Well. Some things you just can't control," I say.

CHAPTER 15

Home

I WOULDN'T MIND going to Adventure Camp again, but let me tell you: there's nothing better than coming home to your own comfy bed and your video games and your backyard tree and your purple teddy bear that nobody knows about because you're in fifth grade and there are some things you just have to keep private.

"Did you have a good time?" Mom asks when she picks me up from school.

"Yeah. It was great."

"Not too cold?"

"We managed." I know she wants to ask me if I had an accident, but for some reason, she doesn't. She just smiles at me in the mirror, and I nod. Sometimes, success is best announced without saying a word. I am in fifth grade, after all, and Mom has to stop asking me about dry nights at some point.

THINGS THAT CANNOT HAPPEN WHEN I'M 40

"I'm glad you had a good time," Mom says. "I have good news, too. Guess what we bought today?"

"What?"

"Tickets to Paris! Aren't we lucky?"

We go to Paris *every* Christmas to visit Papa's family. So every December, fifty thousand adults tell me how lucky I am. I guess they're right, but all I can think of now is kicking off my shoes and reading my *Calvin & Hobbes* in front of the fireplace in my good old home.

"Paris is nice."

"Correction," Mom says, "Paris is the best!"

"But I'll miss my bedroom. And my friends. And fifth grade."

"I thought you said everyone in fifth grade was mean."

"I may have been exaggerating. Fifth grade is complicated, Mom. You can't trust *everything* I say. I'm dealing with puberty."

"Oh."

Mom is quiet the rest of the way home.

Which is okay with me, because I'm busy saving memories.

Acknowledgments

First of all, we must thank the original Francophile and fifth grade comedian, Julien Abdi-Stephens. Without him, Pierre wouldn't exist. Julien is an inspiration, a source of humor, and a fan of justice and compassion. There are lots of real-life adventure camps in America, but the one closest to us is the one in Collin County, Texas—and it's <u>true</u> that all fifth graders camp there to learn about nature and explore the outdoors! So thank you, Plano Independent School District, for investing your money and time to support science and kids. Mr. Solomon (the real genius-brain), Mrs. Niece, Mrs. Micek, Mrs. Villalpando, Mrs. Burke, Mrs. Mendelsohn, Ms. Martin, Mrs. Seward, and all of Shephard Elementary: thank you every day, every year, for doing what you do! My sincere gratitude to Reagan and David at Black Rose Writing. Thank you, Amy, for beta reading and sound advice. And so grateful to Kevin, Polly, and Galit for your endorsements. For a lifetime of love and support, we thank Bobbie and Steve. And of course, as always, for putting up with us, *merci* to our Hervé.

~Lori and Trevor

About the Author

Lori Ann Stephens is an award-winning author. This is her first novel for middle-grade readers. Before she became a university professor, she taught children in *every* grade between first and eleventh grades. That's a lot of grades. Lori Ann likes dark chocolate, cats on Youtube, and everything French. She lives in Texas with her family.

About the Illustrator

Trevor Yokochi graduated with a Studio Arts degree from Southern Methodist University's Meadows School of the Arts. He's a painter, singer, and songwriter. This is his first illustrated book for children. He lives and makes art in Dallas.

View other Black Rose Writing titles at www.blackrosewriting.com/books

and use promo code PRINT to receive a 20% discount when purchasing.

BLACK ROSE
writing™